ONE SMALL STEP
FOR MANKIND...

I was maybe two or three inches off the bed, still in a sitting position with my hands reaching out as if to hold my balance. But I wasn't teetering or wobbly; I was absolutely steady. Reaching down, I swept one hand under my backside and confirmed that I was indeed detached from the bed. Realizing what a momentous event this was, I reached for my cassette recorder and drifted across the room toward the workbench where it lay. Punching the Record button, I uttered these historic words:

"Uh, I'm up."

Ace Science Fiction books by Crawford Kilian

BROTHER JONATHAN
LIFTER

LIFTER

CRAWFORD KILIAN

ACE SCIENCE FICTION BOOKS
NEW YORK

This book is an Ace Science Fiction
original edition, and has never
been previously published.

LIFTER

An Ace Science Fiction Book/published by arrangement with
the author

PRINTING HISTORY
Ace Science Fiction edition/July 1986

ISBN: 0-441-48304-6

Ace Science Fiction Books are published by
The Berkley Publishing Group,
200 Madison Avenue, New York, New York 10016.
PRINTED IN THE UNITED STATES OF AMERICA

Once more,
for Anna and Maggie

1

THE FIRST TIME I ever lifted, I was half-asleep and I nearly broke my neck.

It happened one morning in October. I was asleep until the first jet of the day boomed past over the house. We were about a mile from the end of the main runway at good old Hotchkiss Air Force Base, and the noise was pretty bad.

This time, though, it didn't quite wake me up. I heard it; I recognized it as a T-33 trainer; and I dozed off again. That was when Marcus stuck his big, black, wet nose in my ear.

Marcus is a black Labrador who hates to see anyone in bed when he's already up and thinking about breakfast. As an alarm clock, he's sloppy but effective.

Between the T-33 and the dog, I was pretty nearly awake. But not quite. I was in a middle state, what they call twilight sleep, and I started dreaming about the jet whose rumble was just starting to fade. I imagined myself going to the window, pushing off the sill, and shooting up into the sky in pursuit. I was going fast, and the ground was far below me; I could see the whole town of Santa Teresa spread out below me, and off toward the Sierras was the silver gleam of the jet. I couldn't feel the wind, but I could feel something—something odd but comfortable. It was a kind of tension, a pressure that enclosed me like the swirling water in a Jacuzzi; it held me up and pushed me at the same time. I wasn't afraid of falling, but one side of me was cold. I shivered and turned, and then I was cold all over.

I woke up enough to realize my blankets had slipped off. Marcus was scuffling around. I opened my eyes and saw him backing out from under the blankets, which were in the middle of the floor. The floor was six feet below me.

I was floating horizontally, six feet above the floor and wearing nothing but my Jockey shorts and a horrified expression.

Marcus got clear and looked up at me. Before he even had time to bark his disapproval, I said something clever like "Oh!" as I dropped straight down.

It amounted to a bellyflop onto a hardwood floor, cushioned only by a couple of blankets; Marcus's good reflexes had gotten him away from ground zero just in time.

I lay there for a few seconds, did a cautious push-up, and got to my feet. Marcus sat down at a safe distance and waited to see if I was going to do anything else. All I did was sit down on the edge of the bed.

The one thing I absolutely knew was this: I had been wide awake for at least two seconds before I fell. Whatever had happened to me hadn't been a dream; it had probably inspired the dream. My knees and ribs hurt, and one wrist ached.

"Rick?" It was my mother, Melinda, out in the hall. "You all right?"

"Yeah. I fell out of bed."

"My God, it sounded like a bomb. It's after seven." I heard her slippers slapping down the hall toward the stairs.

Rubbing my sore knees, I looked around the room. As usual, it looked like a bombed-out electronics shop. Opposite the bed was my workbench, running the whole width of the room. It still looked funny with the computer missing. The bookshelves were jammed: manuals, magazines, paperback novels. Where the bookshelves didn't cover the walls, I'd put up planet posters: Jupiter, Io, Saturn. When I pulled the blankets back onto the bed, the floor was littered only with the usual debris—boots, runners, camping gear I'd been meaning to put away since August, the frame of a TV set I'd started building after they took my computer.

Nothing different. No pulleys in the ceiling, no trampoline where the bed should be.

I got up and did an involuntary Groucho Marx glide across the room, my knees hurting. From the filing cabinet where I kept my clothes, I dug out a pair of jeans and a blue-and-red striped Rugby shirt. Tucking them under my arm, I went out and down the hall to the bathroom.

After a quick shower and shave, I dressed and tried to lift again. Nothing. Just a tall sixteen-year-old with wet brown hair, standing in the middle of a bathroom trying to float up into the air, like everybody else does when they're ready to face the day.

On my way downstairs to breakfast I tried to think what Gibbs would say. He'd probably get out Occam's razor: whatever happens, explain it with the simplest theory that fits all the facts.

The simplest theory was that I had had a world-class hallucination. Any other theory would involve junking some comforting basic natural laws, like gravity, and Gibbs wouldn't rush to do anything like that.

Never having had a hallucination before, I had no idea what it was supposed to feel like. Somehow it didn't seem right that a mental misfire could wreck your knees and sprain your wrist.

No: it had happened, for reasons that escaped me completely. Very likely I would never know what they were, any more than a bee understands why it can't fly through a glass window. But it was pretty interesting.

The kitchen was empty. In the adjoining study, where Melinda had her office, she was already at work. I looked enviously at her computer, a beefed-up IBM PC I was legally forbidden to go near.

"You sure you're okay?" she called. I put bread in the toaster and got out the eggs.

"I gave myself a hell of a thump, but I think I'll live." While the eggs fried, I gave Marcus a dog biscuit and let him out into the backyard.

"I think it was because I had a flying dream just before I woke up."

"Uh-huh. They're fun," she said a little absent-mindedly. Her face had a greenish cast from the video monitor. "Done all your homework?"

"Every last little bit. I didn't even use my calculator to do the math."

"Are you bragging, or feeling sorry for yourself?"

"Both."

"Tough bananas."

"Hey, if I can't get a little sympathy from my own mother, I'll run away from home."

"Promises, promises. Let me know when you're going so I can rent out your room."

"Who'd want to live in that dump?"

"A homesick auto wrecker."

Normally I'd have gone along with her mood; we razz each other a lot, and sometimes it's even funny. But my wrist hurt and I was afraid my brain had been sprained even worse. So I just growled and finished eating my eggs. Melinda went on working, building a new house on her video screen.

"Hey, Rick?"

"Uh."

"How you getting along in school these days?"

"Fine."

"I mean with the other kids."

"Fine."

"Bring some of your friends around one of these days. For dinner or whatever. This place gets lonely with just you and me, and you always fooling around in your room."

"Sure."

"Any girls you're interested in these days?"

Aha. If I hadn't been so distracted I'd have seen it coming. I got up and started on the dishes. That was the price I paid for being able to keep my own room the way I wanted it. "Melinda," I said, "am I a male chauvinist pig?"

"Not as bad as some I've known."

"Well, okay, remember that I've been raised by a no-crap feminist, right? So when I tell you that the girls of Santa

Teresa are world-historic airheads, you won't say I'm just a male jerk."

"Not out loud I won't."

I popped the dishes into the drainer. "The guys aren't much better."

"I'm not asking you turn *gay*. But now it sounds like you're not a male chauvinist, you're an IQ chauvinist. An intellectual snob."

"I know enough about IQ testing to know that the people who design them are as dumb as the people who believe in them. Uh, let's change the terms of this discussion, okay?"

"Sure," she agreed innocently.

I dried my hands on a dishtowel and leaned in the study doorway. "Let's say I've got a really high entertainment threshold, and most of these people bore me blind."

"You think some of those little sex bombs are boring?"

I struck like a pit viper. "Now who's being sexist and chauvinist?"

"Touché and shut up." She pushed herself away from the computer and leaned back in her chair. Melinda is a good-looking woman: tall, thick blond hair, blue eyes like lasers. Even in a housecoat, she looked pretty stylish.

"But I worry about you, Rick. I sort of had higher hopes for you than just becoming a computer nerd. You ought to get to know some girls, find out what makes them tick. You're going to end up a lopsided genius. And one of these days, you're going to get a rush of hormones to that big brain of yours. Then you'll probably fall for some *real* airhead because you won't know any better."

"Tell you what," I said. "Suppose I find a girl with a big, handsome, divorced father. Thirty-eight, forty, big muscles, plenty of money, sense of humor, nonsmoker. Can I bring him home, too?"

She laughed, but those laser eyes cooled perceptibly. "God, yes! Better yet, just send him over by himself, and you and the girl can get lost."

That was really a joke. Melinda sometimes had one of her partners over for dinner, or a client, but she had never had a romantic attachment. It wasn't because she was all knotted up about her darling only son, either. She'd always given me plenty of breathing space, and made sure I didn't turn into a mama's boy. No, she just lived a celibate life and seemed comfortable in it. Not happy. Comfortable.

And that worried me. I figured I was having enough trouble coping with adolescence without complicating everything with girls. But Melinda was thirty-five and lived like a nun. It didn't seem quite natural to me, and I thought that for her own good she ought to have a man around at least part of the time. I wasn't hoping for a father figure, either; I had that in Gibbs. But Melinda was my mother, and I loved her, and I thought she deserved to be happier than she was.

Still, even in the happiest single-parent households, you learn to avoid pushing too hard on some subjects. This was one of them, and when Melinda pulled herself back up to the computer I knew I'd been dismissed.

"Your lunch is on the sideboard," she said. "See you after school."

"Right."

As I left the kitchen, I paused for a moment and tried to lift. Nothing.

"Rick?"

I turned; Melinda was looking across the kitchen at me, perplexed.

"Yeah?"

"You okay?"

"Sure."

"You looked all clenched up there, as if you were hurting."

"I was doing isometrics."

Her look changed to standard, exasperated mom. "You know, you're so weird I almost dread to see what kind of girl you'll finally drag home. Go on, get out of here before I call a cop."

I got my school gear together, threw it into a scuzzy old knapsack, and toted the knapsack over one shoulder out to the street where Brunhilde waited.

Brunhilde was my pride and joy: a '69 Volkswagen Beetle, red and dented, which Melinda had bought for my sixteenth birthday. It was a lot like Oscar the Grouch's garbage can only with wheels, but I loved it. It got me around the urban waste-

land of Santa Teresa and up into the hills where I went hiking
most weekends. I suspected Melinda had bought it to make up
for the lost computer; whatever her reasons, I was grateful.

While Brunhilde warmed up, I looked out the windshield at
the willows lining Las Estacas Street, and wondered if I'd
really had a hallucination after all. The street looked exactly
as always, right down to the carved sign on our front lawn:
Melinda Stevenson, Custom Home Architecture. It was
another typically gorgeous California day, with the early
morning sun sending bright shafts through the trees and onto
the lawns. This was a neighborhood of remodelled older
houses; Melinda had gussied up a lot of them, including our
own. It looked so damn natural. Could I really sit in this
rackety bug, on this ordinary street, and honestly believe that
I'd defied the law of gravity in my sleep?

The answer was yes.

2

ONCE I SAW a reprint of a British cartoon from the mid–nineteenth century. A young vicar, a kind of junior priest, is having breakfast with his bishop's family. The bishop says: "I'm afraid you have a bad egg there, Vicar."

"Oh no, Your Grace," says the vicar. "I assure you, parts of it are quite good."

That was how I felt about school.

Santa Teresa High—Terry High to its inmates—was south of downtown, a sprawl of buildings done in what Melinda calls Eisenhower Modern. It was built to hold the first Baby Boomers; the Boomers' babies were still pretty young, so at the moment, the school was underpopulated. In some towns, that might've meant cutting back on the school budget, maybe even shutting the whole school down so some other one could be efficiently overcrowded. But Santa Teresa had a lot of high-tech industries, plus some engineering types out at the air force base; they expected the best for their kids, and they voted.

So what? So we had some programs that would've been blown away as frills in most California towns. That was what kept me from going totally bananas, because one of those programs was the Awkward Squad.

The Awkward Squad was a collection of weird and wonderful adolescents who were practicing to be Nobel Prize-winners or turnips, or both. We had Pablo Sanchez and Ronnie Feinstein, who played almost nonstop chess with each other—without bothering to use a board and pieces. We had Mason Reeves, who played classical violin, jazz saxophone, and professional blackjack—when he wasn't zonked out on dope. We had Eustis Bowson, who rigged up his own LSD lab in ninth grade. We had Angela Battenbury, who was six-feet tall and did calculus in her head. And we had Bobby Gassaway, who ground his own lenses for telescopes and then used the 'scopes to spot flying saucers. Then we had a few others who drifted through on their way to Juvenile Hall or back again, and we had me. I was new in the Awkward Squad, just since September, and in some ways I was relieved to be there. Last year I'd been just your average computer nerd; now I was in the big leagues, nerdwise, even if the computer was gone.

In the Awkward Squad you still had to take some regular courses—Modern Life Skills, English, that kind of stuff—but most of your day was spent in John Gibbs's science lab.

John Gibbs. He scared almost everybody in Terry High, including the principal. He even scared the Awkward Squad most of the time. He was thirty-eight years old, and almost that many feet tall. He was the kind of black guy who tromps through the nightmares of KKKers: big, strong, intelligent, and with the world's lowest crap threshold. When he came into a room, the effect was like nightfall coming behind a thunderhead. Other teachers were into first names and relating to their students. Gibbs called you by your last name, and you called him "Mister" and "Sir" without his ever making a point about it because if you were in his class you weren't totally, suicidally stupid.

As an All-American defensive end at UCLA, Gibbs used to scare quarterbacks, too—right up until the Rose Bowl game in his senior year, when he wrecked his left knee beyond repair. He finished the year, went on to graduate school, and took a master's in psychology to go with his B.Sc. in physics.

Then he took a year's teacher training and went to work teaching high-school science, with a little coaching on the side. In the last ten years, Terry High's football team had beaten the daylights out of every other team in central California. Gibbs was married to the former Letitia Scott; they had two little girls, Flora, 12, and Diane, 10. He owned a three-bedroom house a couple of blocks from school, and was paying off a $75,000 mortgage. He had Visa and American Express cards, and paid his bills like clockwork.

I knew all this because, of course, I'd gotten into his accounts.

Gibbs didn't know it. Nobody did. I'd covered my tracks on that one, and a lot of others.

After leaving Brunhilde in student parking, I headed for the science wing. This could sometimes be the low point of the day, because the shortest route ran along a narrow walk between the main building and a disused portable classroom. This area was known as The Pit, the designated smoking area, and as usual it was full of jerks busy putting a film of tar between their lungs and reality. Apart from the fact that it stank, The Pit was a nuisance because a lot of its denizens had a thing about the Awkward Squad.

Like Jason Murphy. He was a senior this year, by the grace of God and social promotion, and led a little gang who fooled around on Hondas pretending they were Harleys. In the Awkward Squad we called them the Tricycle Rats. That wasn't quite accurate anymore; Jason's father, a car dealer with the dumbest commercials on local TV, was letting him tool around in a demo Trans Am, and his buddies had abandoned their motorcycles for the joy of being seen in a hot car.

I'll say this for Jason: no matter what his problems were, he was blessed with a sincere self-regard. He had an equally sincere contempt for anything intellectual, which for him started somewhere below Conan the Barbarian.

Judging from the smell coming downwind from The Pit, grass was the carcinogen of choice this morning. Jason and a couple of his buddies were sitting on the steps of the portable, all rigged out in the mandatory studded leather jackets and headbanger T-shirts. Jason was a stocky guy, a couple of inches shorter than I, but a lot heavier. He was cultivating a moustache to go with the lank brown hair that lay in oily tendrils down his neck.

"Hey hey," said Jason, genial with cannabis. "It's one of the mutants."

"Naw," said one of the buddies, "it's Mr. Spock. See the ears?"

"Mutant," Jason overruled him. "Get outa here, mutant. This is human territory."

I ignored him, and the smirks of the twenty or so other smokers. As I passed, something stung my neck like a wasp: Jason had flipped the glowing remains of his roach at me.

Feeling the heft of my knapsack, I debated whether to use it as a club, or drop it and go after the three of them with my bare hands. Most of the kids standing around hadn't even noticed, but from the corner of my eye I could see Jason and his friends crouched, waiting, hoping to get a rise out of me.

Down in the basement of my personality, something rattled its chains and growled as it started climbing the stairs. Once or twice, when I was younger, it had gotten out. But I was, as Gibbs once put it, on TV. Under the eye of the authorities, I couldn't afford the luxury of tangling.

So, with my neck hurting, I started walking again, hearing their laughter and cursing silently because my ears were turning red—I could feel them—the way they always do when I get upset or excited. I made a mental contract with myself: as soon as I was allowed to get near a computer again, I would log Jason's name and a lot of phony delinquent accounts into the records of every bill collector in California. Then I would get the registration numbers of his lousy little Honda and his stupid Trans Am, and I would put those vehicles on the "stolen" list of the California Highway Patrol. That would be for starters.

It was a relief to get away from The Pit, and from the gregarious mindlessness in the halls where you could smell the sex pheromones even over the girls' Charlie and the boys' Brut. Once inside Gibbs's domain, I was safe.

That domain was a single large room, with tables and chairs clustered at one end facing his desk and a chalkboard; at the far end, the room held four long lab benches with electrical outlets, gas burners, and sinks. Against one long wall stood eight Apple IIc's, interspersed with bookcases and filing cabinets; the other long wall was windows overlooking the track and football field. Everything was in immaculate order, but the janitors had little to do in here: Gibbs saw to it that we kept the place clean and tidy.

This morning, the lab benches held little gadgets attached to sphygmomanometers—instruments for measuring blood pressure. We'd set them up yesterday afternoon; today we were going to use them.

The Awkward Squad was gathering in the classroom end, talking quietly or reading. Pablo and Ronnie were playing blitz chess, with no more than fifteen seconds between moves, and giggling like maniacs. Eustis was running a program on one of the Apples. Six-foot Angela was hunched over in her chair, devouring yet another junk romance novel with a title like *Love's Palpitating Passion*. She could go through two a day and still keep up with all her work.

Gibbs himself was perched as usual on his tall stool in front of his desk, with a podium beside him. The stool enabled him to keep his bum leg straight; it didn't like to bend very much. He was going through the day's ration of bureaucratic garbage, scanning each item quickly before dropping it in the wastebasket nearby. When the buzzer sounded for the start of first period, he put the remaining papers on the desk and glanced at the papers he'd stacked on the podium. The principal's muffled voice came faintly down the hall from the next classroom. With Gibb's connivance, we'd sabotaged the lab speaker early in the semester; Angela calculated we'd gained an extra ninety minutes a month by that one criminal act.

"Good morning."

The chess game stopped. Eustis left the computer. Angela put away her romance. We all mumbled good morning.

"Good to see everybody on time for a change. Anybody ripped? Anybody drunk?" This was a running gag; he'd made it very clear, on day one, that anyone who got psychotropic before three in the afternoon was no longer in the Awkward Squad. One guy had tested Gibbs; Gibbs had passed, and the turkey was gone.

We all shook our heads at his question.

"Good. It could really mess up what we're doing today, which is exploring biofeedback. Gassaway! What's biofeedback?"

Bobby Gassaway sat up. He was a blond kid about my age, doughfaced, a little zitty, and pervertedly fond of grossly loud sport shirts.

"It's a way to control body functions by conscious effort, sir."

"Good. But it's a strange phenomenon, because you do it indirectly. You don't try to lower your blood pressure; you just try to keep a light burning, or a tone sounding, or a wave at a certain level on an oscilloscope. Now, this morning—"

The door opened, and we all turned to see who it was. It was a girl, a stranger: maybe 5'4", straight blond hair falling across her shoulders, fine pale complexion, hazel eyes, high cheekbones, and a baleful expression. She was very slim, frail looking really, and she wore a gray skirt, white blouse, and blue cardigan. She carried a book bag over her left shoulder; her right hand held a cane, and her right leg wore a brace.

"Can I help you?" Gibbs said.

She held up a handful of forms. "My name is Pat Llewellyn." Her voice was deep, musical, and full of anger. "They told me in the office that I'm supposed to be here."

"Ah, yes—I was told to expect you sometime this week. Come on in and find a seat. I'll take your forms."

She came into the room, limping heavily, and passed the forms to him with scarcely a look. Then she went on to a table off to one side in the second row, away from most of us. I thought she'd have been cute if she didn't have such a grim expression.

Gibbs's rumbling voice pulled my attention back where it belonged. "All right, this morning we're seeing whether we can learn to consciously raise or lower our blood pressure. Now, this is not just fooling around, people. Biofeedback can be dangerous as well as helpful. I've got some notes on carrying out this experiment safely, and I want you to read them before we get going."

He left the stool and started passing out the handouts. As he approached Pat Llewellyn, she said loudly and coldly: "Is that supposed to be a joke?"

"I beg your pardon?"

"If you're doing a cripple imitation, it's not a very good one."

Woo. I figured this girl would have a very short halflife in here. But Gibbs didn't react to the bitter hostility in her voice and face.

"This is no imitation, Llewellyn. This is the best I can do." His voice was quiet and matter-of-fact.

Pat's face tightened into an angry mask, and she flushed with embarrassment as she stared at the empty chalkboard. Gibbs put a handout in front of her, then went back to his stool and sat down with just a hint of relief at being off his leg.

"All right," he said. "After you read the handout, ask questions if you have any. Then we'll pair off; one person monitors the other." He named pairs, preventing another chess orgy by putting Pablo and Ronnie on opposite sides of the lab. "Llewellyn, you team up with Stevenson."

"Who's Stevenson . . . sir?"

"In the Rugby shirt."

I gave her what I considered a medium-friendly smile; she looked at me the way I usually look at a badly dissected frog.

"Some guys have all the luck," Gassaway blared sarcastically.

"Shut up, Gassaway," Gibbs said.

"Shut up, Gassaway," I echoed.

We got ourselves set up after the usual chaos and confusion. I was being a little duller than usual, because I couldn't keep my mind off whatever it was that had happened to me that morning. When I asked Pat whether she wanted to monitor first or be the subject, she put on the cuff and handed me the bulb. I obediently pumped it up and noted her blood pressure.

The first time around, we were supposed to lower our blood pressure. The sphygmomanometer was linked to a small feedback device; when pressure dropped below a specified point, a light atop the device would go on. Pat's pressure was relatively high, which wasn't surprising. She was so tense she almost vibrated.

"This your first day here?" Smooth line, huh?

"Are we doing an experiment or making small talk?"

I shrugged. "Well, the experiment's going pretty slowly, so we might as well pass the time."

Pat glared at me, then at the unlit bulb. "I think this is stupid. And it's supposed to be a science class?"

"Ah," I said. "This is no ordinary science class; this is the Awkward Squad."

She looked slowly around at the other students, who were pumping up each other's cuffs, giggling, and chattering away. "I won't argue with *that*. They told me it was some kind of special science course. I should've realized. When they say 'special,' it always means screwed up."

"Speak for yourself." Witty comeback, huh? "We like to think of ourselves as refugees from a higher plane of reality. Where you from?"

As if reading from a card, she rattled off the names: "Sacramento, Riverside, Sacramento again, Bakersfield, San Bernardino, Fairfield, now here. Name a hole west of Nevada, I've been there."

"Your family travel a lot?"

"Not with me, they don't. They gave up on me years and years ago. I kicked around some foster homes. Now I'm doing group homes. You know? Two underpaid bleeding-heart social workers pretending to be parents, and six jerks pretending to be human."

I started tinkering with the innards of the feedback device. It was simpler than I'd expected.

"Why'd your folks give up on you?"

"I kept asking nosy questions about things that were none of my goddam business."

Pretty salty. "No, you didn't."

"Oh, no?"

"You're too smart to ask dumb questions. You asked smart questions, and you were smart enough to tell when they gave you dumb answers. They're the dumb ones, and they couldn't handle you."

That was no Sherlock Holmes deduction, but it was close enough to the truth to make her nervous. I pumped up her cuff for the umpteenth time. Still high. "Listen to the great expert," she jeered.

"I'm not an expert," I answered mildly. "But you're *here*."

"So what? You said yourself, this is the Awkward Squad."

"That's what *we* call it. The school calls us 'severely gifted.'"

"Severely—" She rocked back in her chair, laughing.

"They don't really know what the hell to do with us, so they stick Gibbs with us and he tries to make something out of us."

"You mean," she asked incredulously, "everybody in here is really smart?"

"Not really smart. Just smart enough to get into high-quality trouble. Gassaway, for instance—he used to get his jollies going around giving everybody electric shocks. Last year he hot-wired the p.a. system. Mr. Gordon, the principal, nearly got electrocuted. Zap, Gassaway's here. Pablo and Ronnie are always playing chess, and they don't care whether they're taking a pee or everybody else is singing 'The Star-Spangled Banner.'"

She studied me with a flicker of interest. "And what are *you* in for?"

"I broke into a bunch of banks up in Canada."

She caught on much too quickly. "Computers, huh?"

"Yeah."

"You steal anything?"

"No. I just liked to leave graffiti. You know, Stop Nuclear War, Bring Down Interest Rates. My favorite was If You Attempt to Erase This Message, All Your Records Will Be Erased."

She laughed again. It was a little harsh, as if she didn't get much practice. "And what did they do when they caught you?"

"Took away my computer and put me on two years' probation. I thought at least they'd offer me a job, you know, showing 'em how to stop other hackers. They said they already had enough crooks on the payroll."

She laughed once more, more easily, and the light went on.

"Hey, you did it! Keep it up, keep the light on."

"How? I don't know how—"

The light dimmed and went out as her blood pressure rose. I felt Gibbs coming up behind me.

"Just think about making the light go on, Llewellyn."

She focused on the light bulb, and then relaxed a little; if I hadn't been watching her so closely, I wouldn't even have noticed. The light went back on, and brightened.

"Well done," said Gibbs warmly, and she glanced up at him with a surprised half-smile, as if she hadn't expected a compliment.

"But how am I doing it?"

"If we knew that," Gibbs said, "we'd know a lot about ourselves. Some parts of our brains can do absolutely astounding things. Sometimes, with the right kind of feedback, we can get some conscious control over them. It's a useful tool, but it can be dangerous."

"Dangerous how, Mr. Gibbs?" she asked.

"Well, as the handout said, you could theoretically push your blood pressure so low you'd go into shock. But the problem's more complicated than that. You understand how your liver works?"

"No."

"Nobody does, really. So you wouldn't want to fool around with it, would you? Control what it was producing. Next thing you know, you could mess up your whole body chemistry and drop dead."

"But if I fooled around," I interjected, "I could learn how my liver works."

"By trial and error? You'd have to be awfully curious to risk your neck like that."

"I wouldn't be the first. Plenty of scientists have experimented on themselves."

"They were taking calculated gambles on the basis of known data. Interfering at random with your own internal functions would just be stupid."

I didn't agree for a second, but I let it pass. Pat didn't.

"You want to know everything about everything," she said. "Don't you?"

"Eventually," I admitted. "Mostly, I just don't like secrets. Information ought to be free, like air and water. That's why I asked you about yourself."

She looked startled, and the light went off abruptly.

Gibbs frowned. "Hey, your blood pressure shouldn't go up so fast." He checked her cuff, then the gauge. "It's hardly gone up at all. Maybe you've got a defective machine."

"Uh, Mr. Gibbs—I kind of tinkered with it."

He impaled me with his the-last-time-was-your-last-chance look. "What now, Stevenson?" Gibbs said very slowly.

"Uh, well, I could see her blood pressure was a little high, sir, and she was under some stress being new in the class and all, so I just made the device a little more sensitive. So it would react faster to even a little drop in pressure, you know, give her some positive reinforcement, and bring her pressure down some more."

"Do you think that was advisable, Stevenson, especially in the light of what you just read about sudden drops in blood pressure?"

Boy, I was skin diving in the deeps of the Excrement Ocean. "I, uh, said that her blood pressure was already a little high, sir, so that didn't seem like a likely threat."

The cuff's Velcro patches gave with a *zzpp* as Pat yanked the cuff from her arm. "So you were just manipulating me, huh? Very clever. Excuse me, Mr. Gibbs, I've got to go to the john."

She stood up and headed for the door, her cane thumping.

Gibbs leaned against the edge of the lab station and studied me with distaste. "See what I mean about tinkering with complicated systems? You haven't been using this device fifteen minutes, you're already messing with it, with no idea in the whole blessed world what might happen next. You call that scientific?"

"Not exactly, sir. Well, in a way I knew exactly what the results would be."

"Uh-huh?"

"I could see how to change the sensitivity threshold, and I could see that I wasn't going to get results with her unless I did change it. And that's what happened."

"But did you know what Llewellyn's reaction would be when she learned you'd been tampering with her just like the machine?"

"Uh, no, sir. But I wouldn't have said anything about it if you hadn't noticed how her blood pressure went back up."

"For tomorrow, Stevenson, I want you to be able to recite from memory the Nuremburg Convention on the use of human beings for experimental purposes."

"Where am I going to find that, sir?"

"That's your concern, Stevenson."

I figured I was getting off lightly, but I had to risk getting into trouble again. "Mr. Gibbs, can I ask you a question about this gizmo?"

"Go ahead."

"I've read that they can help you produce different kinds of brain waves, like alpha waves."

"If they're set up properly, with electrodes on your scalp."

"I'm interested in that. Could I do my project on it?"

He looked suspiciously at me. "You looking for a new thrill, Stevenson, inducing alpha waves?"

"No, sir. I want to induce twilight sleep."

"What on earth for? You suffering from insomnia?"

"No, no—I just thought it would be something interesting."

"Why twilight sleep?"

"Oh, I don't know. It's just an interesting mental state. You know, being able to control your dreams, that kind of thing."

"Stevenson, I've got a bias. It's taken a good two and a half billion years of evolution to produce conscious intelligence. Too many of the people who get it want to get back down among the oysters. Now you tell me you want to *work* at getting semiconscious. That doesn't sound like you, Stevenson. You seem to like staying wide awake. So what's your ulterior motive?"

"None, sir!" I replied, lying like a rug. "But I've read somewhere that it's fairly easy to induce twilight sleep, and I thought it would make a manageable project."

"I don't buy it. You could build the device, but I don't like the idea of you fooling around with your brain, any more than your liver. Find something else."

I nodded, ticked off because now I would have to do some other project as well as the biofeedback. At that point, Bobby Gassaway came over.

"Hey, Mr. Gibbs," he said, "I wanted to ask you about my project."

"What is it, Gassaway?"

"I'd like to do something on UFOs."

Poor Gibbs. He sighed and patted Gassaway's flabby shoulder.

"Give me a break, Gassaway. Last year it was dowsing and spoon bending."

"Yeah, well, I think I can do something really good on UFOs, Mr. Gibbs."

"Gassaway, I don't care what you wash it with, garbage is still garbage."

"Aw, that's not the scientific attitude, Mr. Gibbs. My dad's an air traffic controller, for Pete's sake, and he's got an open mind on the subject."

"Open mind" on this subject meant "hole in the head" as far as Gibbs was concerned, but he was relatively tactful. "Gassaway, this project is supposed to be a little more than clipping stories out of the *National Enquirer*. This is an attempt at a serious scientific project, with reasonable goals and strict methodology. I'm not interested in UFOs because they have nothing to do with science."

"Well, just 'cause something is paranormal doesn't make it wrong, does it, sir?"

"No, Gassaway. Being paranormal just means being safely outside the limits of scientific study."

I injected myself into the discussion. "What would you accept as evidence for something like UFOs, Mr. Gibbs?"

"Direct observation," he answered instantly. "Repeated under controlled conditions, with no chance for cheating. And no ordinary explanation that fits the facts."

"So if I wanted to prove something like UFOs—"

"Not you, too, Stevenson!"

"No, sir! I'm just asking."

"Give me photographs, preferably of little green men."

"Or telepathy?" I went on.

"Tell me what I'm thinking, ten times out of ten. Then do it with a lot of other people." He looked at us. "Now, what are you two going to do your projects on?"

"Well," I said, "I'd still like to do something on biofeedback."

"Okay. Build a device, from scratch. Just for blood pressure, like these. But no fooling around with brain waves, understand?"

"Yes, sir."

Gibbs turned to Gassaway. "If you've really got to do something on flying saucers, you can design a questionnaire and survey all the traffic controllers out at the air base. Find out if they really think UFOs exist, and on what evidence."

"Aw, hey, Mr. Gibbs, I've got all these books—"

"Survey only, Gassaway. Garbage in, garbage out; remember?"

It would serve Gassaway right, I reflected, to have to pester a lot of grown men who didn't want to waste their time on some high-school kid's science project. At least I could go home and get to work undisturbed.

Pat Llewellyn came slowly back into the room. "Mr. Gibbs," she said, "could I speak to Stevenson by myself for a minute?"

"Sure." Gibbs moved off, with Gassaway tagging along. I looked at Pat, who stood leaning on her cane a couple of feet in front of me.

"I don't like being manipulated," she said calmly. "Even for a good cause. Don't ever do that to me again."

"I'm sorry," I said. "I was just trying—"

"Don't. Don't try. Don't be a nice guy or a pal or a jerk. You just get on with your life and let me get on with mine, okay?"

"Okay," I said. "And I really am sorry."

She settled in her chair, ignoring my apology. "Now it's your turn. But first show me how to reset this gadget."

I was chauvinistically but pleasantly surprised to find that she understood a good deal about electronics. Once I'd told her what to look for, she readjusted the threshold herself with no fuss.

"I built myself a stereo once," she said. "That was in a foster home. The guy—the husband—knew a lot."

I studied the light bulb, which stayed off. "Gibbs told me to build one of these from scratch, as a semester project. Want to join me?"

She nodded, but she didn't seem ecstatic. "You'll have to supply the workshop," she said. "Where I'm living now, there's no room. Besides, it's a zoo. I wouldn't leave anything

lying around there; some of the kids are really destructive.
How about your place?"

"No problem," I said.

I couldn't believe my luck.

3

LATER THAT MORNING, the Awkward Squad split up and went to various other classes. I spent an hour ignoring English literature and thinking about the events of the day.

I knew I had lifted myself, somehow, six feet above my bedroom floor. It had not been a dream or a hallucination; my knees and wrist still ached. My mental state, I speculated, might have had something to do with the lift. Certainly my waking up had ended the experience. Trying to repeat the lift while wide awake had failed thoroughly.

So if I could do it again, I'd probably have to be in twilight sleep. That was a problem. How could I do something in my sleep that I couldn't do wide awake?

A thought occurred to me: suppose it happened again while I was asleep on a camping trip up in the mountains? I could wake up and drop fifty feet, or five hundred. Maybe I would have to tether myself to a rock, as if I were a balloon.

But why would conscious thought interfere with whatever it was that enabled me to lift? Maybe it was the kind of skill that worked best when it was virtually automatic, like walking, or driving a car. If you *think* about what those skills require, you only confuse yourself, like a toddler or a learning driver.

I had stayed up in the air for a second or so before realizing what had happened. Only then had I fallen. Ergo, my amazement and panic—not my being conscious—had ended the lift. In a stupid sort of way, I had behaved like all those cartoon animals who chase each other off cliffs.

If I could just get into twilight sleep, and then lift while knowing I was going to wake up, I might be able to sustain the lift while fully conscious and able to enjoy it.

That would be a project I would love to spring on Gibbs. He could observe me to his heart's content. He could photograph me, videotape me, bounce radar off me. I'd call it the bootstrap effect. No—I'd call it the Stevenson Effect, with capitals.

More problems. Supposing I could reproduce the Effect at will, and impress the pants off Gibbs and the Awkward Squad, what would happen next? I realized I'd read too many junk novels about people with wild talents: the army would appropriate me, bury me in some supersecret installation, and keep me there until the whole 82nd Airborne could dispense with parachutes. Or the CIA would just terminate me to keep the KGB from kidnapping me. Or would I become some weird celebrity, doing my thing on TV? Maybe I could do half-time routines at football games. Imagine rising above a crowd of thousands, everyone gazing up in amazement and awe, cameras clicking, flashbulbs going off . . . and some looney drawing a bead on me with a high-powered rifle.

As soon as I thought about it, I knew it would happen. The country was crawling with psychopaths, sociopaths, religious maniacs, and trophy hunters, with the combined firepower of a medium-sized army. All the nuts who were planning on killing a cop, or the president, would instantly vote me Target of the Year. If the archangel Gabriel himself were to appear over the U.S.A. to sound the Last Trump, he'd be shot down before he could get through the first two bars.

That thought cooled me off the whole idea for a while. Whatever the Effect was, it wasn't worth dying young for. I was twitching with eagerness to find out more about it, but I could see that I was going to have to move really cautiously.

For the time being I would have to operate in complete secrecy, but I would also have to document whatever I did— or Gibbs would give me the chewing-out of my life.

By lunchtime I was a quivering mess of anxiety, frustration, and self-importance. As usual I headed back to the lab; the Awkward Squad had to share it with other students, but at lunch it was our property, a refuge from the Jason Murphys and all the other airheads. On my way, I met Pat in the hall.

"Hi," I said. "Come and have lunch in the lab. That's where we all hang out."

"I can't. I've got to get outside. Being inside walls for too long makes me jumpy. In a manner of speaking," she added dryly.

"Want to go off campus? We could go up Hillside to the park. It's got a nice view."

She gave me a cautious smile. "Sounds good."

We walked slowly out to the parking lot. Pat moved in an awkward, rolling limp; I had to gear down from my usual Ichabod Crane stride.

"I sure felt like a jerk after I blew up at Gibbs," she said.

"He'll get over it. Underneath that tough exterior is a gentle, caring, understanding sadist."

"I make myself mad when I pop off like that. I don't have enough self-control."

"Have some of mine," I offered. "I'm so repressed I bore myself to death."

Jason Murphy and the rest of the baboon troop were elsewhere, so we got through The Pit with little more than some giggles and some stares at Pat's brace. She didn't seem to notice; it wasn't unusual for her to be the new girl with the weird leg.

We got into Brunhilde, which Pat took completely for granted, and drove off campus. Pat ignored the endless dull condos and garden apartments, preferring to enjoy the Bach cassette I put on the tape deck. (I like Mozart better, but I was playing it safe; she was definitely not into rock, and would probably consider the nineteenth-century romantics a bunch of schmaltz merchants.)

When we got to the park, she cheered up. We walked from the parking lot across a broad green lawn between stands of aspen and pine, to a row of picnic tables at the top of a little cliff. From there we could look out across the town, past the air base, to the yellow foothills and the black-and-white peaks of the Sierras.

We sat at a table, sharing my lunch (Melinda usually packed enough for three starving longshoremen), enjoying the breeze and the sunshine. A jet taking off made a silver glint against the sky. My small talk evaporated; she didn't seem to mind. After a while she said:

"Thanks."

"You're welcome, I guess. What for?"

"Bringing me up here. I don't get out in the air very often. It's just one damn box after another."

"I get cabin fever if I'm inside too long. So I go hiking almost every weekend—camp overnight if I've got the time."

"Where?"

I pointed toward the foothills. "Out there."

"By yourself?"

"That's the whole idea."

"Boy, you're lucky. D'you get scared?"

"No. As long as you don't step on a rattler, there's not much that can hurt you."

"I'd be scared witless."

I looked at her. "How far can you walk on that brace before you poop out?"

She looked back at me, surprised and almost ready to get sore again. "Farther than you might think."

"Okay. I'll take you up San Miguel Creek some time."

"How far is that? To hike, I mean."

"Hardly anything. Six, eight miles round trip from the road."

"You're on." But I could see from her face that she'd never walked that far.

"Great." I would wait a couple of weeks, I decided, before setting a specific date for the outing.

"Rick—tell me something." Now she was using my first name; we were making real progress.

"How come you're being such a buddy? You just feel bad about fooling around with the biofeedback machine?"

I almost laughed in her face. Suppressing the urge, I said,

"Terry High is a very friendly school. We all like to make new people feel right at home."

"Oh, can it, would you? It's just another lousy small-town high school with a million cliques and no style. I've been kicked out of better ones."

"Okay, I confess. You're not as tough as you pretend. You're a lot like Gibbs that way. I think he must've spotted you for a phony right away, which is why he didn't kick you out on your ass this morning. You're a nice person. I like you."

I know, I know—I was being savagely uncool, as only an amorous nerd can be. All I needed to complete my disgrace was to hand her a bouquet of wildflowers.

But she wasn't feeling so cool herself. I looked into those hazel eyes and I saw a girl who was tired of being alone, a girl who really needed to be liked. What was more, I did like her.

For just a second, I saw her defenses go up; she nearly got off some wisecrack. Then she must have decided the hell with it—a compliment, even from a juvenile delinquent nerd, was better than the proverbial poke in the eye.

"I like you, too."

She reached across the table and put her hand on mine for just a second. Her fingers were long and slender and cool.

4

It was a busy afternoon. In study hall I went to the library and found the Nuremburg Convention that Gibbs had ordered me to memorize, after a lot of searching through the microfiche catalog. The Convention had been worked out after World War II, when the Allies had learned of the experiments on human beings in concentration camps. It was easy to see which of the ten principles Gibbs had in mind:

The voluntary consent of the human subject is essential. The experiment should yield something for the good of society, something that can't be obtained otherwise, and shouldn't be random or casual. The experiment should be designed to avoid all unnecessary physical and mental suffering and injury. And the subject should be free to end the experiment at any time.

Once I'd digested all this, I indulged myself in a little resentment of Gibbs. Did he think I was some kind of baby Nazi, running life-and-death experiments on Jewish prisoners? All I'd done was to tinker with a gadget to make it a little more sensitive. I was willing to confess to being a manipulative smart ass, but I wasn't in the international-criminal class just yet.

On reflection, I decided Gibbs was just using the incident to get me to think a little about the ethical questions involved in such experiments. Talk about manipulative!

Next I went hunting for data on levitation. We had plenty; the shelves bulged with books about telepathy, precognition, psychokinesis, dowsing, and reincarnation. I could imagine what Gibbs must say in staff meetings about library spending.

The stuff on levitation was pretty dumb: saints who were seen (usually by just one person) to rise off the ground while praying; swamis who suspended themselves horizontally with one hand lightly resting on the end of a staff, like a dirigible moored to a tower; spiritualist mediums who occasionally soared aloft during seances.

I didn't believe a word of it.

Well, I could buy the idea of levitating in a trance; I'd done something like that. But it was always supposed to be a religious or mystical ecstasy that got people airborne. When Marcus had poked his nose in my face this morning, I'd been about as mystical as a box of cornflakes. The authors, in any case, were wildly ready to believe and transmit the dumbest stories, with virtually no evidence except the opinions of other authors.

Maybe some of the stories had a basis in fact. If so, the original lifts had been buried in a mass of embroidery, exaggeration, and outright propaganda. That was a sobering thought. I didn't want to end up shot, and I also didn't want to end up as Saint Richard the Flying Hacker, or Guru Rickaswami, or the leader of some weird cult.

The last class of the day was gym, where as usual I was picked last for somebody's basketball team. Running up and down the court while my teammates ignored me, I at least got some exercise and a chance to compile a shopping list.

After a quick shower I found Pat in the hall and offered her a ride home.

"Thanks, but I'd rather walk. If you're going to take me hiking, I'd better get in shape."

"Well, give me your phone number. I'll call you tonight

about the project, and we'll work out a time when you can come over."

She hesitated. "Let me call *you*, after I've cleared it with Morty. He's the house father."

"Fine," I agreed. "I've got to get to my job now, but I'll be home a little after six."

"Then I'll call around seven-thirty or eight." She gave me a cautious smile and walked away.

Driving to work, I reflected on the fact that I was now just another jerk looking forward to a phone call—I, who normally *made* phone calls, and to some of the smartest computers in the country.

My job was over on the north side, in the industrial section of the city. For two hours every day, I worked as a stores clerk for Preuzer Electronics, a wholesaler supplying most of the high-tech firms in town. Willy Preuzer was a sharp old guy, a relic from the days of vacuum tubes, who'd stood by me when the cops ended my life of crime.

"Not because you're a nice kid," he said then. "Because you know your way around the warehouse better than anybody else, even me."

That had been one of the nicest things anybody ever said to me.

Willy was alone in his tiny office when I came through the side door.

"Got a minute?" I asked.

"Sure, sure. What?"

"I want to build an electroencephalograph and hook it up to a biofeedback device."

Willy was a stocky guy in a loud sport shirt; his bald scalp was mottled with sunburn that made the fringe of white hair look all the whiter. He looked up at me from under his bushy eyebrows.

"The biofeedback device is no problem. But the EEG is complicated."

"I only want to pick up theta waves."

"You got insomnia?"

Everybody was asking that question today. "No, just a project. We've got all the parts in stock, Willy. Could I borrow them to put one together, and then bring them back in a couple of weeks?"

"Hell, no. You can buy the parts wholesale. What d'you think this is, the public library? I'll take the cost out of your salary. When you're finished, I'll buy the parts back for the usual prices I pay for used."

I did some rapid calculations. At the very least, this was going to cost me a couple of hundred dollars—a lot more if it turned out I needed the EEG on a continuing basis and couldn't return the parts. But in the glory days, I'd dropped two hundred a month on software alone sometimes; since then I'd had little reason to spend my pay, so I was relatively affluent.

"It's a deal," I said. "You can start taking the price out of my salary as of last week."

"Deal," he echoed, and stuck out a stubby hand. A shake was all the contract he needed. "Now get to work. We got a bunch of orders for Waterby."

I headed for the warehouse with a handful of order forms; a quick scan of the microfiche index reminded me of where some of the items were, the few whose location I hadn't already memorized. As usual, the two hours went quickly. At six, once I was on my own time, I started filling my own mental shopping list, trundling up and down the aisles with a supermarket shopping cart that filled up rapidly.

"What do you need an EEG for, anyway?" Willy asked as he locked up the place for the night. He helped me lug my new acquisitions over to Brunhilde.

"It's a school project."

"A school project. You're spending this much in high school, how you going to afford college?"

"That's what my mother keeps saying. Thanks, Willy— see you tomorrow."

Melinda was home, but busy in the kitchen; I got my gear up to my room without a lot of tedious "but-momming." Marcus observed the whole business, but kept his mouth shut. The new stuff blended in with the old stuff—in fact, I knew I'd be able to cannibalize earlier gadgets for parts of the EEG. Then I washed up and went down to dinner.

"How was your day?" The daily debriefing was under way.

"Pretty good. We're doing biofeedback in Gibbs's class. He told me to build a biofeedback device."

"Interesting," she said, loyally but insincerely. "What's it going to do?"

"Generate a light and a tone when I get my blood pressure where I want it." I paused. "I've got a partner for the project."

Melinda's antennae picked up everything. "A girl? The giantess?"

"No, Melinda, it's not Angela. A new girl named Pat Llewellyn."

"She nice?"

"Kind of a bitch, actually, but she's pretty smart."

"Aw, Rick, you gallant devil, you sure can pick 'em. Is this another of Gibbs's lame ducks?"

"What other kind does he have? Matter of fact, she *is* lame —she wears a brace on one leg."

Melinda put a hand to her mouth, instantly contrite. "That was dumb of me. What's her problem?"

"The leg is the least of it. Actually, she's pretty nice under all the b.s. You'll like her."

Melinda hammed up the astounded-mother act, waving her napkin around. "Don't tell me you're bringing her home to meet me already!"

"I don't have a choice, Melinda."

"Meaning—oh God, am I going to be a grandmother already?"

"Oh, give me a break," I whined. "She lives in a group home, so she's coming over here to help me build the gadget."

"Fair enough. When?"

"I don't know. Maybe tonight."

"Rick, the place is a total mess! How could you invite—"

"Hey, the place looks fine. Just relax, okay?"

Well, she growled a bit more, but the prospect of having me bring a girl over was too enticing. I washed the dishes while Melinda chased Marcus out of all his favorite flopping places with a vacuum cleaner. It was a doomed effort: Marcus inevitably ended up in a freshly vacuumed spot where he promptly shed half a bushel of wiry black hairs.

Pat called just after seven-thirty, and about all she said was: "Come and get me, please." From the uproar in the background—loud rock plus a couple of girls screaming at each other—I could understand why she didn't feel like curling up at home with a good book.

Marcus came with me; he was glad to get away from the vacuum cleaner. We drove over to Pat's place with Marcus sitting up in the back seat, his nose stuck out the window just behind me.

The house was a rambling ranch-style suburban nothing, on a neglected lot behind some eucalyptus trees. Rock music was audible from the street, thumping so hard my sternum started to vibrate when I got to the front porch. I had to press the doorbell several times before anyone heard me. A short, slender, harassed-looking man opened the door; he was wearing jeans, a button-down shirt, and an amazing, bushy hairdo.

"Hello, I'm Rick Stevenson. I'm here for Pat."

"Oh, right. The science project, right. *Pat!* Would somebody turn down—Pat!"

She materialized behind him, wearing a UCLA sweatshirt and bellbottom jeans that concealed her brace. She carried a notebook—more for looks, I suspected, than for use.

"Okay, be back by 10:30 sharp, okay?" Morty said.

"Sure," said Pat. "See you then, Morty. Thanks."

We walked out to the car. "That place is going to drive me insane," she said between clenched jaws. "It's just nonstop. Screaming, tantrums, the music, Morty and Joan—oh, what a great dog!"

Marcus gave her an energetic sniff-over as she settled into her seat; she rubbed his ears, and he tried to crawl into her lap.

"He's gorgeous. I love Labs. What's his name?"

"Marcus Aurelius."

"The philosopher king?"

"We were hoping for just another calm, cool stoic. It didn't work out that way."

I nearly burst out laughing when we got home. Melinda had oiled and dusted all the furniture, and changed into elegant blue slacks and a cream silk blouse. If Pat felt taken aback by the sight of such an elegant matron, she didn't show it. I'd been right: they liked each other on sight. With Marcus escorting them, Melinda gave Pat the grand tour, with detailed technical analysis of all the remodelling she'd done to the house and special emphasis on the study and the computer. They were just getting into a cozy girlish discussion of architecture as a profession when I intervened.

"Let me show you what we have to do tonight," I said.

"Sure," said Pat, but I still had to wait for another burst of "thank-yous" and "delighted-to-meet-yous" before we got upstairs.

Pat shook her head when she saw the high-tech chaos of my room. "I sure hope you know where everything is," she said. "If I put something down in here, I'd never find it again."

"No problem," I assured her.

"Where do we start?"

"We're starting with the biofeedback device. Gibbs gave me a schematic; it can be hooked up to a sphygmomanometer at school, or whatever."

"Or whatever?"

"Well, I'm planning to use it for something else as well. I've got the stuff to build an electroencephalograph."

"This is part of the project, too?"

"No, this is a personal project. You don't have to get involved in that part of it if you don't want to."

Her curiosity was piqued. "What's all this about? You've got a shifty look all of a sudden."

Dramatic pause. "I want to create theta waves."

"Explain."

"Well, the brain produces different kinds of waves, right? Alpha waves are usually associated with relaxation, meditation, all that kind of stuff. Some people buy biofeedback devices because alpha waves can also reflect a kind of high."

"But that's not the kind you were talking about."

"Nope. Beta waves are what we produce when we're concentrating on something. Theta waves show up when we're almost asleep, or in a kind of trance."

"So why d'you want to zonk yourself out?"

This was the part I'd have to be careful about. Pat's crap detector was set on a hair trigger. "You can get some remarkable ideas when you're in a theta state. I've read a lot about it, and I've found I get a lot of good ideas when I'm going to sleep or waking up. So I want to see if I can induce the state more often."

"But this isn't part of the project."

"Gibbs doesn't like the idea of fooling around with the brain."

"I don't think I do, either."

"Fine," I said agreeably. "Just the biofeedback device then. I'll do the EEG on my own."

"Okay. Let's see the schematic."

The evening went quickly. Pat learned fast and asked good questions. By a little after ten we had the main components in place; a few more hours and we'd have a working device. I found it odd but nice to work with a partner instead of on my own. Melinda wandered in from time to time (I ostentatiously left the door open), and we all chatted as we worked. It was a pretty agreeable evening.

The only problem was that I was dying to tell Pat and Melinda why I really wanted to build the EEG, and I knew I couldn't; they'd both think I'd gone completely loopy. They —and I—would just have to wait until I could demonstrate lifting. That might be forever.

I got Pat home just before ten-thirty; the rock music had quieted down a little, but it still sounded bad. Pat only shrugged.

"You got me out of the worst of it. Thanks."

Feeling like a zero-defects idiot, I leaned forward and gave her a kiss on the cheek. She looked at me and grinned.

"You can do better than that."

She was right.

5

IF YOU'RE HOPING for some steamy sex scenes, eat your heart
out. Why should I embarrass Pat (and myself) just to give you
some vicarious jollies? Besides, you'd be much better off
going out for some jollies of your very own.

What I *will* tell you about the next few days is that they
were a lot of fun. We built the biofeedback device in three or
four nights, and spent a Saturday testing it. It worked like a
charm, with a sphygmomanometer borrowed from Gibbs.

Pat and Melinda got along almost too well. By the end of
the week Pat was coming straight home with me and spending
her afternoons in the study with Melinda, fooling around with
her IBM PC and helping make dinner. Toiling away in Willy
Preuzer's salt mines, I might have felt resentful except that I
was coming home and pigging out on homemade pizza, spa-
ghetti carbonara, and lasagna.

"I had a foster mother last year who was into Italian cooking," she told us. "If I could just get the right families, I could
learn to cook anything."

Morty and Joan seemed relieved to have her off their
hands; they could spend more time with the other girls, and

from what I saw of them, they needed all the help they could get. After a couple of phone calls from Melinda, Morty decided we were safe enough for Pat to stay with us until midnight, at least on weekends.

That meant more time to work on the EEG; as I'd hoped, Pat carried right through onto it. But it was a lot more complicated than I'd expected. A whole week's work had to be redone when I made a stupid mistake in wiring, but by then Pat was so efficient we took only two nights to repair the damage.

We talked a lot. She told me about her family: a mother who died young, a father who farmed her out to grandparents while he drifted from job to job and then into a marriage with a woman with children of her own. They tried a blended family; it didn't work. Pat hated her stepmother and stepsisters, and her father didn't help matters.

"He'd just get drunk. So Eleanor and I would fight until we couldn't see straight. Finally she told Dad it was her or me. My granddad was dead, and my grandma was in a nursing home, so I ended up in a foster home as a problem child."

"How old were you?" I asked.

"Thirteen."

"How many foster homes were you in?"

"Six. Can you believe it? I was a real drag in most of them. When I turned sixteen this summer, they figured I might do better in a group home, so here I am."

We were working in my room, with the EEG in its early stages scattered all around us. I don't know which bothered me more, what she'd said or the calm way she'd said it. I guess whatever happens to us when we're kids seems natural, so we take it for granted even if we don't like it. But it sounded weird to me. I'd lived in Santa Teresa all my life, and in this house for the last ten years. I didn't have a father, but school was crawling with kids from single-parent families; at least I had a mother who hadn't died on me, or thrown me out of the house at thirteen.

The brace was thanks to a congenital hip defect that left her leg too weak to support her.

"It hurts," she told me on a drizzly Sunday. "But I guess I'm used to it. The brace is a nuisance, but it sure beats crawling around on my belly like a reptile." Then she changed the subject.

Sometimes I talked about myself, but I didn't think I was very interesting except for one thing that I couldn't talk about at all, at least just yet. It was more fun to compare tastes in music (hers was more highbrow than mine, but neither of us could stand rock) and books (she got a kick out of historical novels; I liked science fiction). Once or twice, when we went out to rent a movie at the video shop, we got into half-serious squabbles that ended in Monty Python as a compromise.

Okay, it was not your typical teen romance. No polite small talk with parents, no cruising the main drag in a Trans Am, no sock hops, no substance abuse. Just a couple of misfits messing around with soldering irons.

In school, I noticed Gibbs was relaxing a lot, getting positively mellow, and realized it was partly because I was being less of a pain in the ass than usual. The Awkward Squad accepted Pat without much fuss, and I even had to give up an occasional evening with her because she'd been invited to Angela's. (*That* was a sight! Pat barely reached Angela's shoulder.)

It wasn't all sweetness and light. One morning, I'd picked Pat up and driven her to school, and we were passing through The Pit. Jason Murphy and his buddies were there, playing grab-ass and showing off their biceps tattoos. He saw us coming and started walking around in circles, doing an exaggerated limp and then falling against one of his friends.

"Oh, Ricky," he cooed in a falsetto, "what would I ever do without you, you big strong stud you?"

"Jason, get professional help," I said. Dumb. He'd gotten a rise out of me, and now he'd try for more.

"Professional help. I don't need no help. Hey, tell me, when you two are gettin' it on, where's the brace go?"

My basement tenant came up the stairs in two jumps, kicking open the door and slavering for blood. I felt myself shuddering; my peripheral vision vanished, so I seemed to be looking down a long tunnel at Jason's smirking face. I have a memory of yelling something, but I have no idea what it was. I took a swing at Jason; he blocked it easily, and the next thing I knew something smashed into my cheek. I staggered back,

and saw Pat on the edge of my narrowed vision. She'd
reversed her cane, and was holding it near the rubber tip.
Jason, ignoring her, was coming toward me, his narrowed
eyes fixed on my face.

Pat swung her cane like a croquet mallet, cracking Jason's
shin. The change in his expression, from ferocity to surprise,
was so sudden I burst out laughing. He yelped and hopped,
grabbing his shin with both hands. That was when Pat hooked
the handle of the cane around his other ankle and threw him
on his ass.

The other denizens of The Pit started cheering and whis-
tling. Jason's goony friends just gaped at their glorious leader.
Pat limped over to Jason and looked down at him.

"You hemorrhoid, you're damn lucky you've still got those
ugly front teeth. You watch your manners, and stay away from
us."

One of the regulars in The Pit, a big blowsy girl, laughed
hoarsely. "Right on, sister! Jason, after this you pick on somebody your own size—like a cockroach."

"Come on," I muttered, taking Pat's arm. The monster was
back in the basement; I was still shaking, but not the same
way. Pat obeyed reluctantly, and I could feel her arm quivering, too. We were both out of our skulls on adrenaline.

Once we were in the main building, Pat started a breathy
giggle. "My God, Rick, that felt good! I wish I'd hit him
again."

I stared at her, and saw a bright fierceness in her eyes,
something like the anger she'd shown her first day in class,
but this time it was happy.

"For God's sake," I protested. "You could get arrested for
assault with a deadly weapon. And now you've made an
enemy out of the biggest jerk in the school."

"He's made an enemy out of *me*," Pat retorted. "I'm not
scared of him. Besides, what are you bitching at me for? You
started it."

"I what? Hell, Pat, I never touched him, and he damn near
broke my jaw." Now that the excitement was dying down, I
could feel it, too: my right cheek was getting puffy, and the
inside of my mouth felt ragged. I'd had no idea my teeth were
so sharp.

"You stood up for me." The brightness in her eyes softened. "My hero."

"Who do you think you are, Olive Oyl?"

She squeezed my arm, and laughed. I didn't feel like joining in. I'm a lover, not a fighter; Pat could do both, maybe, but not an uncoordinated klutz like me. That was why I kept the damn monster locked up in the basement: it could get me into trouble, but not out of it.

I spent the rest of that day expecting some kind of retribution. Jason would jump me in the locker room, or I'd be summoned to the principal's office and find my probation officer there as well, wanting to know why I was getting into brawls. Nothing. Jason was very scarce, and the principal was as always intent only on interrupting classes with the p.a. system.

The story was all over school within minutes, of course, and when I met Pat for lunch in the lab I found her surrounded by half a dozen girls (including a couple of *cheerleaders*, for heaven's sake) eager to make friends with the fastest cane in the west. They took the trouble to compliment me for my part in the fracas, but I didn't feel like any knight in shining armor; I felt like the guy who sweeps up after the horse. Looking at the incident objectively, *I* had been rescued by *Pat;* klutz though I was, I still had enough male ego to feel embarrassed.

No, that was not a good day. Afterward, I started parking Brunhilde off campus, just so we'd avoid The Pit, and Pat agreed it was just as well. But she clearly enjoyed her new notoriety, and I found myself on several evenings having to work by myself because she was off socializing with this or that new girlfriend.

In some ways that was okay. I got to feel sorry for myself a lot, which can be fun, and I also got a little time to myself to think things over.

If all went well, I would be able to use the EEG to put myself into a theta state and then to lift again. If I did it, it would be a major event in scientific history. I wasn't boasting to myself—well, not entirely—but I knew that since the only other such episodes were miserably lacking in evidence, I would have to make my lifts predictable and observable. That meant some rehearsals and practice, before I was ready to go public, but even those practice lifts would be scientifically important. I knew Gibbs would expect meticulous notes and records, and I didn't want to go into scientific history as a talented idiot.

Consequently, I had already started keeping a kind of diary, mostly just recording progress in building the equipment, using a little cassette recorder. It was easier, at the end of a long day, to speak a few words into it than to write something down, and I didn't want to risk putting anything on paper. But who's likely to pick up one cassette out of dozens and play it?

Meanwhile I had also been trying to lift under my own steam, so to speak. In the morning; in the evening; in the shower. Nothing. Sometimes, though, I would get a funny kind of feeling, a sense of something *moving* all around me, an endless wash of energy. Actually, it felt like being in a Jacuzzi only with no water, if that makes any sense. That feeling was all the encouragement I got; it wasn't always enough. More than once, I decided I'd been dreaming after all, that I'd gone into debt with Willy Preuzer out of sheer stupidity, and I was compounding that stupidity by wasting my time building an EEG.

Nevertheless, I had to admit that building the thing was fun, and keeping me off the streets. So by the beginning of November the EEG was completed.

My first trial was on a Saturday morning. I had to use this gunky paste to stick the electrodes to my temples. The EEG was connected to the biofeedback device, which was now rigged to turn its light on whenever it picked up a theta-wave signal.

Everything worked, but I got nothing. How was I supposed to think myself into a trance, for Pete's sake? I kept at it, watching the little bulb until I grew bored and started day-dreaming.

The light went on. And off. And on.

Every time it glowed, I snapped into a beta state of quivering concentration. Gradually, though, I found myself relaxing even when the light grew brighter. It stayed on; I kept it on. After a while the light was only one thing among many on my mind. Sometimes I was in my room, sitting on the edge of my bed with electrodes stuck to my head like Frankenstein's monster's kid brother; sometimes I was somewhere else. I imagined all kinds of things, with memories and fantasies all mixed up. I dreamed.

Strangely enough, it was a jet flying overhead that reminded me of what I was trying to do. I imagined following it as I had on that first morning. The sense of energy swirling around me became stronger than ever; it would have frightened me if, in my detached condition, it hadn't seemed perfectly natural, a quality of life like sunlight or rain that I'd somehow never noticed before. By thinking about it I could make the energy move around me, the way you become aware of your toes by thinking about them. I imagined the energy flowing under my legs and backside, concentrating there. The bedsprings creaked faintly.

I lifted.

This time I was aware right from the start. I was maybe two or three inches off the bed, still in a sitting position with my hands reaching out as if to hold my balance. But I wasn't teetering or wobbly; I was absolutely steady. Reaching down, I swept one hand under my backside and confirmed that I was indeed detached from the bed. Realizing what a momentous event this was, I reached for my cassette recorder and drifted across the room toward the workbench where it lay. Punching the record button, I uttered these historic words:

"Uh, I'm up."

Dolt! I had weeks to prepare, and that's what I came up with. Theta states are great for right-brain work, but lousy for left-brain operations like language.

I was now at the end of my tether, so to speak; the electrode wires wouldn't stretch any farther. I saw that the light still glowed. I drifted back toward the device, my knees still drawn up. Then I rose, slowly, until my head bumped the ceiling.

What I'm not getting across is the absolute naturalness, combined with intoxicating weirdness, that I felt as I lifted. Maybe people who gain their sight after being blind from birth feel something like it: the sudden acquisition of an impossible power, a power everyone dreams about but can't imagine actually having. My bed, my workbench, the bookshelves all looked perfectly okay from an altitude of eight and a half feet;

my feet, floating off the floor, looked equally normal.

The sense of energy flow, of the Effect, was sharper than ever, and I could even see the hair on my arms fluff up a little. I reached up and felt the hair on my head drifting around a little, but not in the fright-wig way it does in an electrostatic field.

For some time I moved very, very cautiously, keeping my feet under me so that if I fell I wouldn't bang myself up again. I commented into the tape recorder once in a while, but just to say things like, "I'm straightening my legs. I'm turning right." Once I even let myself touch the floor, and then lifted back up again.

About then, I noticed that the light had gone out. I was out of theta state, and still airborne. With a reckless tug, I pulled off the electrodes and let them fall to the bed. I stayed up, wide awake, so beta-state I was nearly hysterical.

Freed of my tether, I moved across the room and back again, stopping myself before I hit a wall or bookshelf. Next I turned a slow somersault, straightening out and ending up horizontal, about two feet below the ceiling. I noted that I still had inertia, just like an astronaut in free fall, and it took a conscious act of will to put on the brakes by altering the energy flow around me to absorb my momentum. Otherwise, I would have crashed into the walls like a diver hitting the bottom of a shallow pool. How did I do it? I decided to move in a certain direction, and I moved; I decided to stop and I stopped. Not instantly, but quickly enough to feel the tug of my own inertia.

Within a few minutes I was tired, but not from lifting. My muscles kept clenching up on me, the way they do when I'm in a dentist's chair, and I had to remind myself to relax. Finally I settled back onto the bed. The sensation of energy faded, but not entirely. It was there, rippling over my skin like the faintest of breezes, needing only my conscious wish to bring it back.

"Rick—lunch!"

I twitched and blinked and realized I'd fallen asleep for almost an hour.

"Coming, coming." I staggered to my feet, feeling fuzzy-headed and clumsy. Melinda was already going back downstairs; I trailed after her into the kitchen, which was full of the aroma of chile con carne.

"You sure were quiet in there," Melinda observed as she handed me a bowl of chile. I settled into my usual chair at the table.

"I fell asleep."

"What? I'm not going to put up with your burying yourself up there if you're not actually doing something constructive. I've got plenty of jobs for you if you can't find any for yourself."

"I know, I know. I was lying on my bed thinking about the biofeedback device, and I just nodded off. Must've stayed up reading too late. I'll get to the chores as soon as I'm finished here. Could I have another bowl, please?"

"If you can walk to the stove and serve yourself."

"I guess I can manage that." And I could.

"What's with Pat these days? Haven't seen much of her."

"She had a lot of homework, so she went over to Angela's to do it with her. We might go out to San Miguel Creek with Marcus tomorrow."

"Marcus will be delighted, but is Pat up to it?"

"She says she is."

"You've got a tough customer there, Rick. I didn't think you had such good taste."

"Thanks a lot. First I get harassed because I don't pay attention to girls; then I get hold of one and you tell me you doubted my taste. That's what I get for having high standards. Maybe I ought to start harassing you to hunt up some guy."

"My life isn't complicated enough?"

"I need somebody to take me to baseball games, and show me how to fish. I need a role model."

"Oh, can it!" She'd picked up that phrase from Pat.

"Maybe he'd even mow the lawn."

"Are you saying I'd only attract a dummy who'd let you con him into doing your chores?" She gave me a fond tweak on the ear that would've rated as aggravated assault in any court in the country. "Speaking of the lawn——"

"Say no more. Your whim is my command."

Now, why didn't I tell Melinda right there and then what I'd discovered I could do? The thought crossed my mind as I went down to lunch, and I thought about it some more as I mowed the yard. (November, and still mowing the grass! California has drawbacks.) Partly it was caution—I really wanted to be confident and in control of lifting before I revealed it to anyone.

But mostly it was fear. Not fear that she'd shriek and pass out on the kitchen floor, or anything stupid like that. Fear of our lives changing as I knew they would have to change—suddenly, radically, forever. She was having a good time designing houses and worrying about her weird kid; I'd been having a pretty good time, too, even without my computer. Once I went public, all that would vanish. We might end up rich and famous, but we'd also have no privacy. People would trample over the grass I was now cutting so unenthusiastically, and stare in the windows. Or maybe throw rocks through them. Reporters and TV crews would besiege the place. I'd probably have to drop out of school, at least for a while. Pat would come in for all kinds of corny commentary about playing Lois Lane to my Superman. They'd go after Gibbs, who would not appreciate it.

I wasn't really ready for all that. It made me feel guilty just to think about it. Who the heck was I to turn people's lives upside down?

Quite apart from what it would do to people I cared about, I was also pretty scared about what might happen to me. Those crazies were out there, crooning over their guns and their grievances and ready to compromise, if necessary, by shooting me while I sat in a chair. Or the army might indeed declare me top secret and whisk me off to some lab.

By the time I'd finished the front yard and gone to work on the back, I had a good case for dropping the whole thing. Maybe I'd lift just now and then, in private, as a secret vice. Melinda and Pat could avoid all the upheaval, and so could I.

Halfway through the back yard, I knew that wouldn't work. Whatever the Effect was, it came out of a fundamental quality of the world that no one had even suspected before (not counting saints and swamis). Whatever that quality was, it had to be explored, studied, and understood. Given my compulsive curiosity, I couldn't sit on a secret of this magnitude. I was a security risk even to myself.

Nevertheless, I decided as I dumped the grass clippings into the composter, I wouldn't rush into any premature revelations. First I would learn all I could on my own, maybe for a year or two. Once I was in university, I could tactfully break the news to the physics department.

That wasn't really very satisfactory, but at least it meant I could postpone anything serious while continuing to investigate the Effect on my own.

I put the mower away in the garage feeling I'd accomplished something; as I came out into the driveway, I saw Jason Murphy's white Trans Am cruise slowly down Las Estacas Street. He was behind the wheel, with a couple of his buddies as passengers; they all flipped me the bone and boomed around the corner.

6

FOR ONCE, PAT'S place was dead quiet when I picked her up; it was seven o'clock on a Sunday morning, and everybody else (except Morty) was still asleep. I took Pat's rucksack and walked her out to Brunhilde, where Marcus was waiting with his head stuck out the window and his tail thumping. It was a chilly morning under a dull overcast, and Pat had dressed sensibly: wool pants, a flannel shirt, a wool jacket, and a very snazzy black beret. I worried about her shoes, ordinary runners, but she had nothing better.

"Had breakfast?" I asked as we drove east out of town, past the air base.

"Tea and a bagel."

"I'm glad I brought a lot, then. You'll need it."

"Don't be so patronizing."

"Huh? I'm not being patronizing. I just know—"

"Can it."

"I'm sorry."

She made a face and shook her head. "I'm sorry, too. I shouldn't have barked at you like that. Especially when you're taking me out like this. I just get so damn depressed sometimes, living in that zoo."

"I know." I did, too; I'd been invited to dinner there once.
Yech.

"And another year and a half of it before I graduate, if I
graduate."

"You'll graduate," I said, surprised.

"Not if I flip and bug out of there. Find a job somewhere
and live on my own. I could at least make enough money to
go to community college."

"You're acing all your courses right now," I reminded her.
"You should be able to land some huge scholarship to Cal or
Stanford, and then you can be really independent. All you
have to do is tough it out a little longer."

She wasn't in a mood to be cheered up; hell, I'd be
depressed, too, starting the day on tea and a lousy bagel.

"What's the point of university? I'd just come out a bitchy
cripple with a bachelor's."

I'd never heard her call herself anything like that. "Is that
what you think you are? Really?"

"Oh, not always. I just wonder sometimes if it's worth all
the hassle. If I was on my own and doing just a joe job, at
least I'd have some time to myself and some privacy."

This was all scandalizing. "Whatever you want to do with
your spare time, you can do it better if you've got a decent
job, not a joe job. How long d'you think you'd last in a joe
job, anyway? You'd just bug everybody until they fired you,
and you'd be glad to be fired because the job would keep you
trapped with people just like your roommates."

"Yeah." She patted my shoulder. "You ought to be a gui-
dance counselor when you grow up. Don't mind me. I just get
these screaming fits sometimes."

"Uh-huh." I reached into the back seat, where Marcus was
snoring obscenely, and gave him a poke in the ribs to shut him
up.

"What've you been up to this weekend?" she asked, changing the subject.

"Oh, fooling around with the EEG, mostly."

"Getting any theta?"

"Yeah, almost right away."

"You're kidding! Wow, how does it feel?"

"Different, I guess."

"I'll have to try it. Get any good ideas?"

"Millions."

"I'll have to try it. Say, when are we going to bring in the biofeedback device to show Gibbs? He keeps nagging about it."

"Pretty soon," I said. "Maybe in a week or two. I can't run the EEG without it."

"Why don't we surprise Gibbs with the EEG as well?"

I was tempted despite myself. "I'd love to, but he'd kill us. He said no messing around with brains or livers."

"But if we're just creating a theta state, what's the harm?"

"He wouldn't worry about that, I think. He'd be sore because we—because I—did what he said not to."

"You've got a lot of respect for him, don't you?"

Some girls would have said I was scared of him. "Yeah, I guess. Sometimes I think he's too fussy, but if he didn't keep after us we'd all fall apart."

"Speak for yourself," she laughed; then she nodded. "You know, he's the only decent teacher I've ever had. He's a pompous bastard sometimes, but at least he *thinks,* and he expects us to think, too."

"Problem is," I said, "he expects us to think as well as he does."

As we got out of town and into the foothills, Pat's mood improved. She had a couple of Melinda's whole-grain buns (with homemade raspberry jam from our own raspberries) and a little box of orange juice. With her blood sugar up, she cranked down the window to enjoy the rush of cold, clean air. Brunhilde's poor old heater couldn't compensate, but Marcus thought it was a great idea. The two of them nuzzled each other while I drove with freezing hands and feet.

The country here was mostly rolling hills, mostly covered in long yellow grass, with clumps of oak trees here and there. We had the road to ourselves; it climbed into steeper country where pines replaced the oaks. Mist hung in ragged streamers over the ridges.

I turned off on the gravel road that led to San Miguel Creek. Halfway up to the parking area, we saw three deer—two does and a yearling—slip off the road and into the trees. Pat squealed.

"I've never seen them, not wild like that. Isn't that awful? God, they're beautiful!"

Looking at her, I thought she was beautiful, too, but I wasn't about to say so. Her face was pretty, all right, but always tight, guarded; now her guard was down, and she was so beautiful she made me dizzy. I wonder, now, what *I* looked like just then, deep in a spasm of self-congratulation over my insane good luck.

The parking area was at the end of the road at a small, public campsite. The creek ran down out of a canyon, almost inaudible under the rush of wind in the trees. Pat pulled her rucksack straps over her shoulders; I took my own backpack, far larger and heavier. The trail wound along the steep north side of the canyon, not climbing much yet. The chilly air smelled good. I found myself enjoying the slow pace that Pat kept me to, instead of my usual quick striding. We talked, noticed mushrooms and mosses and flowers, and held hands. Far below us, the creek tumbled whitely over rocks. Marcus raced up and down the trail, occasionally checking up to make sure we hadn't gotten ourselves lost.

After a mile or so, I called a halt; the trail would start to climb soon, and I wanted her to rest awhile. We munched on gorp (good old raisins and peanuts), listening to the white noise of moving water and wind.

"That's what it feels like," I blurted.

"What?"

"Nothing. The wind just reminded me of something." What it reminded me of was the feeling of the energy flow, the Effect. I started babbling about hikes I'd been on, just to change the subject. Boy, that had been close. Sitting there, lulled by the noise, I'd nearly gone into theta. The thought of having an unreliable brain was not a pleasant one. Remember, I told myself: she's living in one reality and you're in another.

We carried on, up a gentle grade and over a couple of plank bridges across minor streams. The mist was all around us now, blotting out all but the nearest trees.

"How's your hip?"

"Fine. How's yours?"

But I could see she was tired and hurting, so I called another halt. We perched on a long-dead log, warming ourselves with hot chocolate from my Thermos.

"What does it look like to you?" I asked.

"Different. *In*different. It must've looked like this a thousand years ago. Ten thousand. It'll look the same when we're gone."

"That's partly why I like it out here. Indifferent—that's a good way to put it. Places like this don't care if you're smart or dumb, or good or bad. They don't tell you the rules, but they'll give you a chance to figure them out. If you don't learn fast enough, you get hurt."

"Just like life," Pat said with a smile. She heaved herself up onto her feet. "I've got to go pee. Don't look."

"I won't."

She moved across the trail to a clump of trees that perched on the edge of the slope, blocking the view of the creek. I sat and looked at the ground between my boots for a while, thinking. She took a long time. Then I heard rocks rolling and clattering, and Pat, scared, calling my name.

Jumping up, I ran across the trail and into the trees. The slope within the grove was shallow at first, but steepened sharply and dropped away into something like a scree slope of loose rock and gravel just about at the angle of repose. Maybe a hundred feet down the slope, Pat lay on her back in a cloud of dust. The trail of disturbed rock and dirt was dark brown against the beige of the slope. Right at my feet was Pat's cane.

"Are you okay?" I shouted.

"I think so," she called in a shaky voice. Her feet were pointing downslope. "But I can't move. When I try, I just slide farther down."

Another sixty or seventy feet beyond her, the slope turned into a near-vertical cliff; I couldn't tell how far the drop to the creek was, but it was farther than I wanted to see her fall.

"Don't move." Great advice. I stood on the edge of the cliff and bit my lip. No rope, with us or in the car. Someone might have turned up in the parking lot or the campsite with a rope, but I didn't think a run back down the trail was worth the gamble.

"I'm coming down after you."

"*Don't*. You'll get stuck, too. Just go get help, Rick. Please."

I reached for the feeling of the Effect, and there it was.

Marcus sat there with a worried look on his face, and I worried that he might follow me.

"Stay," I ordered.

I didn't turn up the power; instead, I drifted down the slope, the soles of my boots just tapping the rocks. Pat tried to twist her head around to see me, but couldn't. A good thing, too. I must have looked like Oberon the King of the Fairies, tiptoeing down the hillside. When I reached her, I stopped just behind her.

"Hi."

"My God—how'd you do that? Now we're both stuck, you jerk."

"Nope. I'm going to pull you back up, but I can't move you around, okay? I'm going to grab you under your arms, and you'd better not be ticklish. Then I'm going to pull you up, all right? Just let me take your weight. I'll know where to put my feet."

"I think you're insane."

"Just relax."

So help me, I looked around to make sure no one was watching. Not that anyone up on the trail could have seen anything odd, since we were screened by the grove of pines. Squatting down, I slid my hands under Pat's arms; my feet were just barely touching the rock, resting instead on the Effect. I lifted myself up and back a little bit, dragging Pat with me. She tried to help by shoving her heels into the rocks, but they gave way and she slid back, almost unbalancing me.

"Oops! Easy, easy."

"I'm sorry," she said. "You okay?"

"Yeah. Just relax." I lifted again, and again. The scrape of rock and gravel under Pat's body helped to conceal the fact that I was making no noise at all. A long tongue of mist drifted down the canyon, wrapping us in chilly fog. I found myself observing the Effect under new conditions: it took a lot more effort to lift while carrying extra weight. If I'd had to carry Pat's entire weight, I might not have been able to get off the ground at all.

In just a couple of minutes we were back in the grove. Marcus looked relieved, and gave us a congratulatory thump of his tail. I got Pat's backside onto firm ground and stood up, letting the Effect fade away. Then I helped her to her feet and got her cane.

"What the hell happened?" I asked.

"I came down here to do my business, and when I was finished I got up and lost my balance." She gave me a dirty, make-something-of-it look.

"Boy, you sure scared me. How are you? Did you get hurt?"

"I don't think so. I might have some bruises, but that's all. It was almost funny, you know? Sliding downhill like that." She looked at me more gently. "You must be some mountain climber, to get both of us out of there."

"No, dope, I just watch where I put my feet."

"What a sarcastic rat you are." But her heart wasn't in it. With one hand gripping my arm and the other on her cane, she began to walk back to the trail.

"Hurt?"

"Yeah, a little. I'll get over it."

She did, too. We went on down the trail for a couple of miles, moving at the same slow pace, before we stopped again. On the last stage of the hike, where the trail climbed through a series of switchbacks up the side of the canyon, Pat had a little trouble climbing over the steep, crude steps, but she insisted on doing it herself.

The trail ended in a meadow, not quite high or cold enough to be alpine, but a pleasant enough place that looked down into the next canyon and out toward the west. The overcast had burned off by now, and the late-autumn sun was warm on our faces. We climbed up through dead grass to a rocky shelf, and basked there like a couple of lizards.

"I'm starving," said Pat.

So I dredged out lunch: pastrami on rye with hot mustard, pickles, olives, some of Melinda's industrial-strength potato salad, more hot chocolate, and some of my own trail cookies —a sort of mix of gorp and granola. We finished up with hard green Granny Smith apples that cracked like gunshots every time we took a bite. Marcus contentedly crunched on a giant dog biscuit.

Groaning comfortably as my blood sugar shot up, I tucked

the backpack under my head and stretched out on the rock to soak up the sunshine, with a paperback sf novel to keep the sun out of my eyes. Pat put her head on my stomach, got out her own book (a biography of Nikola Tesla, patron saint of the severely gifted—Gibbs had turned her on to him), and settled down with a sigh.

That was in the middle of a couple of the happiest hours in my life. I didn't worry about anything—not the Effect, not what to say or do about the girl on my stomach, nothing. The sun was hot on my face, and the air was cold. But I knew, once I put the book down and dozed with the sunlight an orange glow through my closed eyelids, that this was the end of my ordinary life. Somehow I just couldn't stir up the energy to be scared or depressed or even serious about it.

"Hey, Rick?"

"Mrf."

"Thanks."

"What for?"

"Bringing me up here."

"Save your thanks until I've got you back down in one piece."

She bounced her head, hard, on my stomach, rolled onto her side, and started tickling me.

7

THE NEXT DAY my life began to get bizarre. I know, I know—
it was already about as ordinary as life with the Kent family in
Smallville, but now it got really strange.

First, Gibbs was grimmer and more preoccupied than usual
on Monday morning. Then he got on my case about the biofeedback device, which he knew shouldn't have taken this
long to put together. I said we'd been running tests on it (and
we had) and would bring it in the next day.

"Let's run some more checks on it," Pat suggested near the
end of the class. "It's kind of fun."

"I can't, not tonight."

"Why not?"

"I've got something else I have to do tonight. Another
experiment."

"Oh?" She was surprised and interested. "Tell me about it."

"I can't. That is, I want to try a couple of things out before
I show anybody."

"Aw, come on. Now you've got me interested."

"Really, Pat, I can't tell you." I'd always considered
myself a pretty fair amateur liar, but here I was, squirming

and smirking and racking my brains to come up with something plausible.

"Something with the EEG?" she asked quietly, so Gibbs wouldn't hear.

"Not exactly. Listen, it's kind of a surprise, okay?"

"Okay," she shrugged, but I saw a kind of caution in her eyes that hadn't been there for weeks. "So just bring in the device tomorrow morning and we'll run it for the man."

About then, one of the typists from the main office came down to ask Gibbs to see the principal (the p.a. system in the lab was still sabotaged). He was gone some time, and came back looking powerfully unhappy. He practically kicked us out, and took off for the gym office.

By lunchtime, the word had reached even the Awkward Squad: Wes Powell, our star offensive back, had gotten himself bunged up in last Friday's game with Modesto. X-rays showed he had a broken ankle and would be out for the season.

I thought it was too bad. Wes was a nice guy, and I envied him his fantastic speed and coordination. I didn't have anything against football, as such; it just seemed to be a loud and uncomfortable way to waste your time when you could be breaking into Canadian banks instead. But I also knew I was hopeless at that kind of athleticism, and therefore a poor judge of the significance of Wes's broken ankle.

As I walked around the halls, though, I kept overhearing people who talked as if Wes had been shot by snipers. Some of the football groupies were actually sobbing in the cafeteria. I overheard a couple of tubby little tenth-grade guys lamenting.

"Geez, how we gonna beat San Cristobal without Wes?" said one.

"We're gonna get killed," the other moaned. "You know what? The last time Terry High lost to San Cristobal, I was in sixth grade. Now we're gonna get killed."

In English lit, Mr. Pryce couldn't keep his mind on *Lord of the Flies* (who can?), and kept trying to cheer everyone up by pointing out that it's unhealthy to put too much stock in winning all the time. The idea is to play as well as you can with the ability you have, he said. The idea didn't go over well.

At lunch, Pat and I sat in the lab with Angela and Bobby Gassaway, listening to him go on and on about his UFO project.

"My dad says they get UFOs on the radar all the time," he asserted proudly. "I've interviewed him and three other controllers. They all agree."

"I'll bet Gibbs will love your report to death," I predicted. "All a UFO is, is a flying object that hasn't been identified. So it's an airplane or a glider or a balloon."

"Some of these bogies don't act like ordinary aircraft," Gassaway insisted.

"Shut up, Gassaway," I riposted wittily.

"Let him talk," Pat said. I shrugged and rolled my eyes, as tolerant as the next guy if the next guy was in the Spanish Inquisition.

Actually, I didn't mind letting Gassaway carry on, but it was a little annoying to have Pat come to his defense. I was beginning to suspect she might be sore at me because I was doing something without her, and that in turn seemed like a pretty intolerant attitude on her part.

After lunch I daydreamed through a couple of classes, planning my night's activities, and ended up in gym. It was the usual semimilitary grab-ass, with lots of calisthenics to warm us up, and then some basketball on the outdoor courts.

As usual I was chosen last, for a team playing another one led by Jason Murphy. I'll say this for Jason: for an obnoxious twerp with a negative IQ, he played pretty good basketball. He and his guys waxed us to a high gloss in no time at all. Then, somewhere in the middle of the game, somebody tossed the ball to me and Jason fouled me.

Actually, what he did was to slide one foot between mine and trip me so I fell forward. I hit the court with all the grace of a trunk full of crockery, and got up sore. Jason was down at the far end of the court, grinning and dribbling.

Without bothering to say "Shazam!" I turned on a little lift and shot down the court after him; it was an eerie feeling, with my feet barely touching the ground—something like running downhill. Jason made a shot, missed, and went up for the rebound. I slammed into him on my way up, snatched the ball from his fingers, spun around in midair, and took off for the far end of the court.

Now, I hadn't gone all that high, but I still could've hooked my chin on the rim of the basket. Jason may have been surprised; I know I was. In no time at all I was back under our basket, jumping, and doing a pretty fair slam dunk. Coming down was rough; I turned off the Effect once I'd launched myself, and nearly stumbled when I hit the asphalt.

"Way to go, Stevenson!" one of my teammates said. That was about the highest praise I'd ever received for an athletic feat, so I shot out and stole the ball from Jason again. The ball nearly got away from me a couple of times as I dribbled back —I was still an uncoordinated klutz—but the end was the same.

Inside five minutes, we'd turned the game around. In the adjoining court they'd stopped playing to watch. Every time I went in for a layup and then lifted, the guys on my team started yelling.

By the time the game ended, we were too far ahead to count. Jason tried to foul me a couple of times, but I was too fast for him. As we left the court, headed indoors for the showers, I saw Gibbs standing on the track nearby, beckoning to me.

"You were looking good, Stevenson."

"Thanks, Mr. Gibbs."

"How long you been jumping like that?"

"Oh, gee—I dunno."

"You look like you've been practicing a lot. How come you haven't gone out for anything this fall?"

"I'm not really into sports, Mr. Gibbs. You know that."

"Do you know how fast you were running?"

"No, sir."

"Take a lap."

"Aw, hey, Mr. Gibbs, I've been running my tail off—"

"You aren't even breathing hard. Take a lap around the track, and make it a fast one."

So I did, giving myself just a little forward push and a little lift. As I went around the far curve I had to fight against the temptation to let go and shoot around the track, or soar into the air. Lifting wasn't scary now; it was fun, and the desire to let it rip was strong. Idiot that I was, I should have realized that Gibbs hadn't just felt like giving me a chance to show off.

So I went pretty fast, sailed past Gibbs, stopped, and trotted back. I was breathing hard now. Gibbs looked at his little digital stopwatch. Surprising him was like surprising an anvil: hard to do, and hard to tell when you've done it. But when he looked up at me, he was indeed surprised.

"Stevenson, come here."

He showed me the stopwatch. "You just ran the quarter mile in 52.5 seconds. That's pretty good."

"Yeah, well—"

"Look at me, Stevenson, and tell me something. I want an honest answer from you."

"Yessir."

"Are you on any form of drug? *Any* form?"

"No, sir."

"I believe you. Now, how long have you been running like this?"

We had attracted a small crowd of jocks and coaches. Some had seen me run, and were telling the others.

"Uh, gee, sir, I've always been kind of fast. I guess I'm just getting it together."

"You're a long, long way from getting it together. You run all wrong. But if you run that fast now, with real training you could break records."

"Ah, well, I don't know about *that*, Mr. Gibbs."

"Somebody get me a football." It materialized like magic; in his hand, it looked small. "Let me see you catch this."

I ran out onto the field. Gibbs threw the football to me, and I caught it the way a nine-year-old girl would, fumbling instantly.

"Again," Gibbs ordered. "Only this time, look the ball into your hands. Keep your eyes on it."

The next couple of throws were a little better. I cleared my throat. "Mr. Gibbs, I have to go. I'll be late for my job."

His face turned grim again. "Who's your boss? Still that electronics guy?"

"Yes, sir. Willy Preuzer. He's a good guy, but he expects me by four o'clock, and it's way after three already."

Gibbs walked off with one of the coaches, talking quietly. The other coach nodded and Gibbs turned stiffly back to me. "Give me your boss's address, and then go shower."

"Huh?" I answered cleverly.

"I need to talk to him."

Believe it or not, it took that long for the penny to drop. When it did, it dropped like a guillotine blade. "Uh, Mr. Gibbs, do you have some idea that I should be playing football?"

"The address, Stevenson."

I gave him the address and he told me he'd wait until I'd showered. Then we'd both go over to see Willy at the warehouse.

When I got out of the gym, I told Gibbs I had to take Pat home and that I'd meet him at the warehouse; he agreed. But when I found Pat and told her what was up, she said not to bother with giving her a lift. "You've obviously got a busy afternoon *and* evening ahead of you."

"It's really no trouble," I insisted.

"Go on, go," she said. But she didn't look all that happy.

Willy and Gibbs were having a merry old chat over a cup of coffee when I got there. They made quite a contrast: the pink-faced little guy with his tonsure of white hair, and the black giant who seemed to fill up Willy's office all by himself.

"So you're turning into a jock," Willy said. "Your Mr. Gibbs tells me you're running four-minute miles."

"Not exactly," I mumbled.

"Stevenson," said Gibbs, "we're trying to work something out so you'll have time to practice with the team at least a couple of afternoons a week. Mr. Preuzer thinks he can arrange it."

"But Willy," I protested, "I need all the work I can get. I still owe you a fortune for the—" I almost mentioned the EEG in front of Gibbs, but bit my tongue in time. "—the gear and all," I ended lamely.

"Don't worry about it," Willy said with a smile. "Listen, if it's just Wednesdays and Thursdays you're off, and maybe some Fridays when you've got an away game, I don't mind. It's just till Christmas anyway, right? Mondays and Tuesdays are always the busiest days. Besides, with Wes Powell out, what are we gonna do against San Cristobal?"

I felt like banging my head against something nice and hard. Willy Preuzer, of all people, a closet high-school football fan!

Gibbs smiled at me. "I think this is going to work out just fine, Stevenson. Tomorrow in gym we'll work on that throw, and do a little running. By Thursday you'll be doing fine." He got up and shook Willy's hand. "Thank you, Mr. Preuzer. I really appreciate your understanding. Would you like a couple of tickets to the game? Get 'em at the gate—they'll be waiting for you. And Stevenson—"

"Yes, sir?" I answered dully.

"Don't forget to bring in the biofeedback device tomorrow."

"No, sir."

That night at dinner, I was great company for Melinda: a bit like having the mummy of Rameses II propped up at the table. She finally couldn't take it any more and clonked me on the head with her soup spoon.

"All right, what's the matter?" she barked.

"I've got to play football," I muttered.

"Well, you don't have to sulk about it."

"You don't understand, Melinda. This is for real, in the game on Friday. I've got to be an offensive back."

Melinda looked off into the distance, trying to decide if I was joking or plain barmy. "Why *you?*" she asked at last.

"I was showing off like an idiot in gym today, and Mr. Gibbs saw me. So he had me run a lap, and I was pretty fast, so he went to Willy Preuzer and there I am."

"I never knew you were athletic."

"I'm not, for crying out loud. I guess I'm just kind of getting my coordination together after all the growing I've been doing."

"And you were so fast that Mr. Gibbs wants to put you in as a back?"

"Even though I catch like a wimp, and I know next to nothing about football except that it can cripple even a big tough guy like Gibbs."

As an appeal for pity, this was a flop.

"I think it's terrific," Melinda beamed. She settled back in her chair, looking at me with a new respect I found absolutely insulting.

"You know even less than I do about football," I retorted bitterly.

"Well, I'll start learning. And I'll be there on Friday."

"To see me get trampled into a pulp. Some of those guys on San Cristobal, they look like trees they're so big."

"What does Pat think about this?"

"I don't know. I told her a little about it, but she didn't say much."

"She coming over tonight?"

"No. I've got some things to do up in my room, to get the biofeedback device working right for tomorrow."

"Okay. I've got to go in to the office this evening; I'll see you when I get home." Melinda shared an office with a couple of other architects; she went in at odd times, rarely more than once a week.

"Sure. I'll clean up the kitchen."

"I should hope so. A back, huh? Gee, I think that's neat."

Neat. I couldn't believe it. My own mother. She'd probably turn up at the game in a Terry High sweater, a little pleated skirt, and a couple of pompoms.

Once she was gone, I washed up quickly and headed upstairs. It was getting dark already. I changed from jeans and a light brown shirt into black wool trousers and a dark blue sweater. Black gloves and a balaclava cap completed the outfit. Even though it was uncomfortably warm in such a get-up, I made myself stay inside the room until darkness was complete outside. Meanwhile, I practiced lifting, moving back and forth across the room with my legs tucked under me tailor-style. When I felt ready, I turned off the bedroom light, opened the window, and lifted.

The window was on the east side of the house, concealed both from the street and from the next-door neighbors by a huge willow whose drooping branches hung within inches of the glass. I didn't even step on the sill, but simply angled up and out, brushing through the branches and out into the cold night air.

Las Estacas Street was deserted and dark. The neighbors, inside their brightly lit rooms, would see only their own reflections if they looked outside. Gaining confidence, I pulled the balaclava down over my face to minimize the chance of being spotted (a pale face or hand can really stand out in the dark), lifted clear of the willow, and rose to a height of about a hundred feet.

That was some feeling. The Effect was just as strong as it ever was in my room, with my bed safely below me. Something more than the chill of the evening pierced through my sweater, though, and made me shiver. I was *outside*, with nothing at all overhead and a long distance to fall if anything went wrong. But looking down at the rooftops and streetlights was exhilarating. The town looked like a model-train village. I went east, still climbing at a steady rate, and headed for the lightless safety of the foothills.

My learning curve was almost as steep as my climb. I discovered that the Effect could push me quite briskly against air resistance; if I wanted to, I could travel in a standing position. But the wind in my face and the flapping of my clothes were uncomfortable and distracting, so I tilted into the horizontal with my head in the direction of travel.

Superman must have known something I didn't: when I extended my arms in front of me, the wind shoved them around and nearly dislocated my shoulders. I tried folding my arms across my chest, and finally just shoved my hands in my trousers pockets to minimize air resistance, and kept my face down.

And what did it feel like, to fly like a rocket through the night sky with my hands in my pockets?

It felt wonderful.

My altitude was perhaps two hundred feet; the top of the Bank of California tower, off downtown, seemed just about level with me. Down below, the streets of the east side slid by quickly. I saw a car and tried to match speeds with it, but it was too uncomfortable: the wind made my eyes water.

I was now balancing myself between two forces—the Effect, and ordinary aerodynamics. If I tilted head-down too much, the wind shoved me down farther; once I flipped over completely in a somersault. If I raised my head and shoulders a bit, the same thing happened and I found myself flying feet-first to glory.

Gradually I got myself organized again, and by trial and error learned the proper angle to assume for a given speed. Once I got the hang of it, it was possible to lift much faster, and I really began to travel. Reaching the highway to the hills, I caught up with a car that seemed to be going well beyond the fifty-five-mile speed limit; then I passed it, cackling softly to myself inside my balaclava. I boosted my speed higher, higher, until the wind was howling in my ears and my trouser cuffs flapped madly around my ankles.

I sneezed, which destabilized me a bit and made my nose run. Trying to blow my nose, I took my hands out of my pockets—and my trousers promptly slid down around my ankles.

"Hey!" I shouted stupidly, and started to slow myself down. It took a lot longer than I expected, but at last I was hovering; I reached down and pulled my pants up, shivering and giggling. Somehow the silliness of it all sobered me up a bit, and I decided to head for home at a more reasonable speed—with my hands in my pockets no matter how much my nose ran.

It was an uneventful trip back, though I was beginning to feel the cold. The lights of Santa Teresa grew closer and brighter. I had a bad minute or two when I found myself completely disoriented, unable to make sense of the lights and streets below me, until I recognized the 7-Eleven on Coronado Boulevard; after that, navigation was dead easy. I dropped gently toward our house, slid through the window, and turned on the lights. I had been gone just under an hour.

Thoughtfully, I changed back into jeans and checked out the biofeedback device. It told me my blood pressure was a little high, but I brought it down in less than two minutes. Then I went downstairs and gave Marcus his nightly dog biscuit.

When Melinda got home a few minutes later, I was sitting at the kitchen table, demolishing a bowl of chocolate ice cream and reading a science-fiction novel.

"Hi," she said. "Quiet night?"

"Pretty quiet," I said.

* * *

The next morning I took the biofeedback device to school. Pat was already in the lab, studying for a quiz.

"All set," I said, plunking the device down on the counter of our lab station.

"Great." She didn't look up.

"Hey—is something wrong?"

"I'm sore at you."

"What for?"

"You're not being honest with me."

"What d'you mean, not being—"

"You told me you had some experiment or other to do at home, but when I called, there wasn't any answer."

"Well, uh—"

"Look, I don't really care *what* you're doing, but I really hate being lied to."

People were drifting into the lab, and ostentatiously staying clear of us—but within earshot. The Awkward Squad was never strong on tact.

"Pat, I *wasn't* lying," I hissed. "I had to go out for about an hour. That was part of the whole experiment, for Pete's sake."

"And just what was this mysterious experiment, Dr. Stevenson?"

"I can't tell you yet."

"Sure. What's the matter—afraid I can't keep a secret?"

"Pat—" I tried to take her hand, but she pulled it away. "I'm sorry, really sorry, if it looks like I don't trust you. But it's—this is—it's just something I'm not ready to tell *any*body yet. Not you, or Melinda, or Gibbs or anybody."

She didn't say anything, but went back to her book. I didn't know what to do. On one hand, I thought she was being silly, overreacting to nothing. On the other hand, I knew she'd grown up feeling betrayed and deserted by everyone she ever cared about, and she must figure I was running true to form. And on the third hand, I knew that if Pat were keeping secrets from me, I'd probably react the same way: I can't stand not knowing things that other people know.

At that point Gibbs arrived like a *deus ex machina* to put an end to my protestations. We demonstrated the biofeedback

device, with each of us lowering our blood pressure, and got a
B+ for the project—down from an *A* because we'd taken so
long. Since that was my fault, not Pat's, I felt really guilty;
with that burden added to my lack of study, I flunked the quiz
with a resounding thud.

Matters got rapidly worse. Gibbs had been pulling strings
like a mad puppeteer, and just before lunch he told me to eat
in a hurry and get out to the field; I was going to spend the
whole afternoon learning how to play football.

It was so bad, I almost enjoyed it as a form of penance. I
rapidly discovered that anything I thought I knew about football from occasional games watched on the tube was wrong.
It's a completely different game from what you see on TV or
from the stands: everything happens too fast, and everyone is
trying hard to wreck one person: the guy with the ball. Gibbs
and the other coaches pulled together a couple of teams from
the regular gym class, mostly to give me practice in being
swarmed all over. I was feeling too self-conscious to lift at
first, so they knocked me on my ass time and again before I
could get away with the ball.

At one point, as I picked myself up, the thought crossed
my mind to just carry on like this for an hour or so more, until
Gibbs decided he'd made a mistake. Then he'd say thanks but
forget it, and send me home. It struck me as the most brilliant
yet obvious inspiration I'd ever had, and a sure-fire way to
keep from being clobbered for the next six weeks.

I wish I could say that my loyalty to John Gibbs, my dedication to Terry High, and my own self-respect kept me from
chickening out. Actually, what happened was that I got a
break as the scratch football team broke up at the end of the
period. The next period was the last of the day, and among the
new recruits for the next teams was good old Jason Murphy.
He ambled over to me, smirking and flexing his muscles.

"Word is you're a turkey," Jason announced. "I dunno what
you were on yesterday, mutant, but today you're gonna get
your ass kicked."

"You watch your mouth or I'll get my girlfriend to beat you
up again."

I said it loud enough for some of the other guys to hear,

and they laughed right on cue. Jason's smirk turned into a
hammy frown.

"You watch *your* mouth," said the master of repartee, and
slouched off.

So it wasn't loyalty or dedication or anything noble that got
me going that afternoon: it was hatred and contempt, plus a
solid chunk of fear about what Jason would do if he got his
hands on me.

Gibbs set up a scrimmage and talked to me for a minute
about how to take the ball from the quarterback and then run
like hell. I nodded, thinking more about whether I'd be able to
hang on to the ball when it was passed to me.

We went into the play, I got the ball and managed not to
fumble it, and Jason came through the line with his wiry, hairy
legs pumping. His lips were skinned back from his teeth, as if
he thought displaying his fangs would scare me. As a matter
of fact, it did.

I took off to my right, and Jason shifted to intercept. Just
before he reached me, I lifted and spun. I was still touching
the ground, of course, but the Effect whirled me around and
away and launched me down the field. Out of the corner of
my eye I glimpsed Jason nose-diving into the turf. Then I
darted away from a couple of other tacklers, outran my own
blockers, and covered sixty yards in not much time. The guys
on my team set up a cheer, and I came strutting back.

"That's more like it, Stevenson!" Gibbs called. "Okay, you
people," he shouted to Jason's team, "you look like Thanks-
giving Day on the turkey farm. Don't you let him outrun you.
Now let's go through it again."

This time Jason came on a little more cautiously, waiting to
see which way I'd break. I loped around the right end while
Jason and two or three other guys closed in. Another burst of
speed and I was clear.

The third time, Jason came on faster than I expected, and I
was a little slow. Just as I was getting up speed, he was right
in my path, diving for my knees. I suppose I could have lifted
right over him, but only by going higher than any normal
person could. So I cranked up the Effect and crashed right into
him.

My left knee, pumping up, caught him on the shoulder and flipped him over and out of the way. The shock was hard, harder than I'd expected, and for a second I was afraid I'd broken my kneecap. But the way ahead was clear, so I went on down the field again. When I turned around, a crowd had gathered around Jason; he was still lying on his back on the grass.

Uh-oh. I had sudden fantasies of Jason crippled for life and suing me for millions. Or Jason dead, and his parents suing me for even more. But by the time I got there he was sitting up, doing a really fine goldfish imitation while Gibbs checked him out.

"Doesn't look like you broke anything, Murphy. Just got the wind knocked out of you. What did you think you were doing anyway, tackling like that with no protection? You could've hurt Stevenson, too." Gibbs glanced over at me.

"I'm okay, sir. I just banged my knee into him kind of hard, I guess."

"Feel okay?"

"Yessir. Jason, you okay?" I inquired insincerely.

"Yah . . . yah." He struggled to his feet, held up by a couple of other guys. Gibbs sent him off to change and check in with the school first-aid office. As he shuffled off the field, the monster in my basement let out a contented growl.

A little later, I was suited up in a proper blue-and-gold football uniform, complete with pads and helmet, and standing around with the varsity team.

The mood wasn't entirely chummy. I knew most of these guys, and they were nice enough; the trouble was, they knew *me*. Jerry Ames, our quarterback, had spent the last few years avoiding being on teams with me, and now he kept staring incredulously.

"C'mon," I overheard somebody say, "Gibbs isn't serious. This is like, to cheer us up, give us a smile, you know?"

That ticked me off. Here I'd just turned Jason Murphy into a hundred and fifty pounds of compost, and these bovines were patronizing me. I stood off to one side a bit, squinting a lot and trying to look cool.

"Hey, Rick?"

I turned and saw Wes Powell hopping across the grass on

crutches, with his jeans split to the knee to make room for his cast.

"Just want to wish you a lot of luck," he said, and shook my hand.

"I'll need it," I muttered, more grateful than I cared to admit for his public support.

Once we got into practice, I was a target again—this time, of guys who could run like mad and who outweighed me by thirty or forty pounds. You might think that Sean Quacken-bush is a funny name, but when its owner was bearing down on you, you stopped grinning because Sean was 6'4", about 220 pounds, and still growing.

We did some running plays first, and I managed to escape being killed by Sean and the others. Gibbs was pleased; I could tell by the carnivorous smile on his face when his best tackles couldn't nail me. Then he got bored with watching me run around the ends, and switched us to plays where I had to go through the line.

What a massacre. I'd get the ball and look for a hole in the chaotic whirl of bodies. Then a solid wall of defenders would rise up out of nowhere and pulverize me.

The fear of Sean Quackenbush was a real incentive to learning how to spot the holes. If I went through them with a little lift, I was able to get past the defenders most of the time; if I landed in front of somebody, a boost of lift threw me into the guy hard enough to get him out of the way.

After four or five of these plays, the whole team got kind of giddy. Guys on both sides were stopping and staring, even when Gibbs bellowed at them from the sidelines. He wasn't alone there, either. A crowd was gathering, maybe a hundred students and some teachers. Mr. Gordon, the principal, showed up. He was a nice enough guy, who put up with more guff from the Awkward Squad than he should have. He was even polite to Gassaway, who'd nearly electrocuted him last year. Now he stood beside Gibbs, a stocky guy with red hair and not much of it, looking like a middle-aged cherub chatting with the Prince of Darkness.

The practice went on. With Gibbs goading them on, the defenders went berserk trying to stop me, and a couple of times they succeeded beyond my worst nightmares. If I went in through the line, they could still catch me in midair and pull me down before I had a chance to boost myself forward. Still, we weren't doing badly, and by the end of the practice everyone was feeling fine. Gibbs gave us a pep talk that dwelt mostly on how we were luckier than we deserved to be to have a half-decent replacement for Wes, and that everybody was going to have to come up with 150 percent on Friday night or San Cristobal would take advantage of my inexperience and wipe us out. I expect his real purpose was to take some of the wind out of my bagpipes, and he succeeded.

Still, I went home feeling pretty pleased with myself, and parked myself in the kitchen to regale Melinda with a grunt-by-grunt account of my exploits while she fixed dinner. She listened in silence, attentive, amused, and a little bewildered.

"This sure isn't like you," she commented when I paused to draw breath. "Did Pat watch the practice?"

"No . . . She's kind of sore at me."

"Why?" She sounded really alarmed.

"If I knew that, maybe she wouldn't be sore. She really overreacts sometimes."

"Ah. Sure. What did you give her to overreact to?"

"Nothing. I'm working on a little project and I said I couldn't invite her over last night."

"What project?"

"Oh, just something I'm fooling around with. Hard to describe without a lot of gibberish. If it works, I'll show you. If it doesn't, I'll cannibalize the components."

"Well, make an effort to patch things up, okay? I'd hate to see you two break up."

"Break up? Who said anything about that?"

I got through dinner, cleaned up the kitchen, and headed upstairs. I ached a little bit from all the exercise and pounding, but the thought of getting out into the night sky made me fresh and impatient. It was one thing to use the Effect to increase my speed and agility on the ground; it was another to make it carry me up into the air, as high and as fast as I pleased.

The phone rang. It was Pat.

"Hi," she said. "I'm sorry I was such a crab. How was the practice?"

"Fine. I missed you." Actually, I hadn't even thought about her. "You ought to come and watch tomorrow. You going to the game?"

"Sure, I guess. What are you doing tonight?"

"Uh, working on my project some more. The experiment."

"Oh. I thought we might study for the calculus quiz together."

Oh boy. I'd forgotten all about it. And after flunking the last quiz, I was going to get serious flak from Gibbs regardless of my late-blooming athletic skills. "I wish I could, Pat, I really do. Listen, let me pick you up early tomorrow morning, and we'll study before class."

In the pause, I could hear Morty bleating: *"Please* turn the music down, girls!"

"Okay," said Pat. "Pick me up about seven-thirty?"

"Will do. I'll need all the help you can give me."

I hung up, feeling a little guilty, and went to my room. There, I spent half an hour reviewing the calculus and then switched to science fiction. The evening dragged. I realized Pat and I could certainly have spent the evening studying together—but we would have taken too long, and I wouldn't have gotten her home until eleven or later. I was waiting for Melinda to go to bed, which would be a lot sooner than eleven.

The evening dragged. Finally Melinda came upstairs from her study a little after ten, peeked in, and said good night.

"Good night," I answered. "I'm sacking out pretty soon myself. Been a hard day."

"Good thinking. My son the jock. I still can't believe it."

She went on down the hall to her room. I waited. Her toilet flushed. Fifteen minutes passed. I finished the sf novel and started another one. Half an hour. She'd be asleep by now; Melinda was a compulsive early-to-bed, early-to-rise type. I undressed quickly, pulled on my lifting clothes, and turned out my light. Two minutes later I was out and up, revelling in the roar of the wind in my ears and the rush of the Effect on my skin.

As before, I headed for the foothills. It was a cold night, but I didn't mind. I goofed around a little, swinging from side to side, diving and rising. That wasn't always fun. I still felt

G forces, so when I dived, my stomach protested the sudden plunge and when I rose, it felt as if I weighed three hundred pounds.

At some point I saw a cloud drift by overhead, and decided to lift right up through it. The Effect shot me upward, fast; the earth dropped away below me. My ears popped, then plugged up again, muting the rush of wind around me. The cloud came toward me, surrounded me, and then was below my feet and dwindling. I laughed; my own voice was faint in my ears. Soon I started panting. The air must be getting thin, I thought vaguely, but it didn't seem to matter. All that mattered was climbing higher and faster, higher and faster.

Somewhere up there, I passed out.

I can't really remember what it felt like. I have a confused memory of being really cold, and I think I dreamed. At some point I was awake again, awake enough to realize I was dropping like a stone—no, like a human being.

I was tumbling head over heels. My ears hurt violently, and the wind slapped and shoved at me. How fast was I going—a hundred and ten, a hundred and twenty? The world rolled up into my field of vision and sank down again. I seemed to hang in a roaring emptiness between the earth and the stars, and a long time passed. I called out, but my voice was lost in the wind. Soon I would strike the ground, and then I would die. It seemed logical, but not something I should worry about too much. It was more important to realize, as I now did, how *big* the world was, and how little I was.

Finally I was back in thick enough air to revive my oxygen-starved brain and make me realize what was going on. I turned on the Effect and felt weight return—a lot of weight. It occurred to me that I could apply the Effect so strongly that I'd break every bone in my body from the G force. Or I could apply it so weakly that I'd hit the ground hard enough to achieve the same result.

Down below was a hillside cut by a canyon, and oaks clustered darkly in the moonlight. The earth was coming up fast now, and I put on the brakes more firmly. Finally, after what seemed like a long, long time, I came to a stop only about a hundred feet above the canyon. The air was thick and sweet; I closed my eyes and panted the way Marcus lapped water.

After a while I looked for the lights of Santa Teresa and headed for home almost on autopilot.

It wasn't quite midnight when I slipped into my bedroom and quickly undressed. Carefully I put my lifting clothes away and slid into bed. Not until I was under the covers did the implications sink in: I had nearly killed myself. I had abused my powers and had stupidly risked death. If I had gone a little higher, or stayed unconscious a little longer, or panicked when I revived, I would now be a smear of exploded protoplasm on some dark hillside.

I was a long time falling asleep.

8

AFTER·A DAY like Tuesday, I needed a peaceful and relaxed Wednesday. Instead, I went to school and found Pat in the kind of mood that starts thermonuclear wars. I walked into the lab, sat down next to her, and said hi.

"I'd like it if you'd sit somewhere else," she said quietly.

"What's the matter?"

"I don't want you sitting next to me."

"Can you at least give me a reason?"

"I don't have to give you a damn thing. Now, you can get up and move or I can get up and move, but I was here first."

"Pat, hey—would you please tell me what's bugging you?"

She gathered her books and got up, moving across the room to share a table with Angela. They talked in undertones for a minute, with Angela nodding solemnly and glancing disapprovingly in my direction.

If I'd been rested and less wound up, I might've been cooler about it. Instead I slammed my notebook open and concentrated on the calculus I should've studied all last night instead of gadding about in the lower troposphere. The hell with her. Here I was, levitating like a saint with afterburners, and an overnight sports hero as well, and she was in a snit over some imagined insult.

Gibbs limped in and took roll. He could see Pat and I weren't sitting together, and my expression did everything except put the story into good English. His own face, however, showed nothing, and he swung into the first topic of the morning: progress reports on projects. His chief victim was Bobby Gassaway.

"Just gimme a few more days, Mr. Gibbs," Bobby begged. "I've gotta go back and talk to all my sources again. My dad says they're picking up a whole rash of UFOs this week, and it's just perfect for my report."

"Is that right," Gibbs droned.

"This is the real thing, Mr. Gibbs. They turn up late in the evening, then they move all over the place and vanish. Last night my dad saw one shoot straight up to eighteen thousand feet and then come back down and disappear."

"I assume this will be in your report, Gassaway."

"Yes, sir, but I really need a few more days. I'm hoping to get a sighting, maybe even a photo, and my dad says he'll try to get a photo of a UFO on radar."

Gibbs sighed almost imperceptibly and nodded. "All right, Gassaway. One more week. Next Wednesday your report will be in, without fail."

"Yes, sir."

I sat back in my chair, shuddering. Eighteen thousand feet, in almost no time at all. No wonder I had passed out; I was lucky not to have been frostbitten as well. I must have been dropping at well over a hundred miles an hour, and a few more seconds' unconsciousness would have left me just a mysterious red splatter on a hillside somewhere.

Irrationally, the thought made me even sorer at Pat. I would have been dead, and she would have nursed whatever her silly grudge was until it finally sank in on her that I was gone forever. Maybe they'd have found my body, or what was left of it, and she could have gone to my funeral. Then she could have spent the rest of her life regretting she'd been so crummy to me. . . .

This was a pleasant enough fantasy, and I wallowed in

self-pity for much of the morning. Then, when the calculus quiz came up, I suddenly remembered I'd promised to pick Pat up at seven-thirty to do some early studying. Instead, I'd slept until almost eight and rushed off to school alone. She'd had good reason to be sore at me.

Guilt and ignorance of the subject matter make a guaranteed prescription for failure on calculus quizzes, and I now had one more reason to feel sorry for myself. I began to wait impatiently for the afternoon and the chance to be a hero again.

At lunch Pat went off with Angela before I had a chance to apologize, so I gravitated to the corner of the cafeteria where the jocks hung out. They gave me a big hello, kidded me about the size of my lunch (Melinda was emptying the kitchen to feed me, on the premise that playing football burned a lot of calories), and generally made me feel welcome. I had a good time, and got some good advice about how the game should go on Friday. Exempted from extra practice, I spent the rest of the afternoon doing English lit and social studies while waiting for three o'clock.

It wasn't exactly the same as the last couple of days. I trotted out in my pads and uniform (number 77) and saw the bleachers half-full of students and teachers and general passers-by. Gibbs and Mr. Gordon were talking to a weedy young guy who was holding a microphone attached to a cassette recorder.

Wes hobbled out onto the field on his crutches and had a good time putting us through warm-up exercises. I did my jumping jacks and knee bends like everybody else, except that I puffed more and got tired sooner. I was used to all-day hikes, but not to sustained bursts of energy, and the other guys were in much better shape than I was. It made me realize that too much reliance on the Effect could lead to real health problems—quite apart from passing out and bumping into the planet at a high rate of speed.

Gibbs came out onto the field and we gathered around him.

"Gentlemen, as you can see, we have an audience of some size. Looks like the word has got around. A couple of the people in the stands are coaches from San Cristobal. We're going to give them a show they'll remember, so they go home and spread despair and depression all over their team."

"Yessir!" we all bellowed.

"All right, let's start with some passing plays."

We did short passes and long passes, and then some really long passes. Jerry Ames and I started really clicking, each anticipating what the other was going to do. Gibbs screamed at the opposing squad to nail me, and they did their best to oblige him. In one play, Sean Quackenbush trailed me down the field and came down on me like divine wrath as I caught the ball. Rather than pivot and evade, I turned on the Effect and shoved myself right at him. The collision sounded like a couple of trucks meeting head-on, especially inside my helmet, and without my pads I'd've been pulped. But Sean bounced off, and I got my touchdown without any more trouble.

The crowd in the stands started cheering. Gibbs sat down on a bench, his bad leg straight out in front of him, and smiled with a flash of white teeth while Mr. Gordon hopped up and down and waved his fists around in the air.

"Geez, Stevenson, how'd you do *that?*" Sean asked as he picked himself up and we headed back up the field.

"Good timing, I guess."

"Well, just remember I'm on your side, remember? Take it easy."

"Sure, Sean. I'm sorry."

We did some running plays after that, including some to make it clear our strategy didn't depend entirely on me. Having a big audience made everybody show off a little: we were big on grunting and shouting and thrashing around a lot. The sun sank and the air cooled, but no one left.

Finally Gibbs called me off the field to rest, and I looked over the stands to see if Pat was there. She wasn't.

After practice, I drove out toward the city airport and parked outside a small shop on Santa Barbara Boulevard. It was called The Junior Birdman, and it specialized in equipment for skydivers, sailplane pilots, and ultralights. A big tanned guy came out of the back room when the door jingled.

"Yeah, chief. What can I do for you?"

"I want to buy an altimeter and a windspeed gauge."

"Getting into skydiving, huh?"

"Well, you know."

He showed me quite a range of devices, most of them insanely expensive as far as I was concerned. Finally I settled for a bare-bones outfit that still came close to bankrupting me.

"Can I interest you in a good jumpsuit?" the tanned guy asked.

"Not just yet."

"What kind of parachute you using? I've got some great ones, on sale."

"Uh, I don't have—I don't need a parachute just now, thanks."

"Okay, chief. Coming out to the meet at the airport next Saturday?"

"I don't think I can make it."

"Too bad. Gonna have some of the best people in California out there. Guys, you'd think they were really flying, y'know?"

"Uh-huh. Well, thanks." I handed him a check that left about six dollars in my account, and scuttled out.

Dinner was quiet. Melinda had a new commission and was already in the high-intensity meditation state she always enters in the early phase of a new job. I ate my tamales and rice and thought about Pat's knockout Italian food. Then, while Melinda immured herself in her study to commune with her IBM PC, I washed dishes and thought confused thoughts.

I knew I was in the wrong with Pat, that I'd behaved like a jerk and hadn't made much of an effort to straighten things out. But I still felt the time wasn't right to reveal my secret, and the secret was more important than anything else right now.

Finishing up the dishes, I went to the phone and called Pat. Morty, shouting over music that sounded like exploding garbage cans, said she was busy and couldn't come to the phone. I asked if she'd call me back, and hung up.

She didn't call back. In penance, I ground away on my calculus most of the evening, took Marcus for a long walk, and got back too late to phone her again. I would just have to see her in class tomorrow.

For once, Melinda stayed up late, working on her new house. At last she went to bed. I rigged myself up with my new gadget strapped to my chest, and five minutes later I was soaring through a deck of low cloud into an emptiness glittering with stars. The dials on my gadget were illuminated, so I could tell my windspeed and altitude at a glance.

It was a strange feeling to be able to put numbers to what I was doing, to know I was five hundred feet above ground level and traveling eighty miles per hour. Eighty miles per hour, and I wasn't even trying hard. After last night's scare, though, I wasn't eager to test my limits. For all I knew, I could break the sound barrier, or even hit escape velocity and go into orbit. Neither was a record I wanted to set.

In any case, I had enough to amuse me. Once into the foothills, I cruised up and down canyons, just above the tree-tops, and balanced on cliffs before somersaulting hundreds of feet down and soaring back up again. The feeling was marvelous. I didn't feel light as a feather, except when I shot up and let myself drop again. No, I just felt . . . powerful. Maybe surfers feel that way. I was getting a free ride from a source of infinite energy; while I could easily hurt myself, it would be my own fault if I did. That knowledge kept my eyes open and my mind alert.

Everything poured in as I glided slowly over the dim foothills. The air smelled good. The wind rustled in the trees, and I could distinguish the noise of every leaf. In fact, my hearing seemed to be unnaturally sharp. An owl launched itself out of the blackness of an oak tree, saw me, and plunged into the shelter of another tree; I could hear the faintest whisper of its feathers. Something squeaked on the edge of a night meadow far below and I could have dropped to the exact spot.

In some ways it was like swimming. I could hover and let the breeze push me gently, this way and that, as if I were inner-tubing down some lazy creek. Once or twice I drifted into a tree, or bumped my way slowly along a cliff face. When I tired of that, I lifted a thousand feet and looked out across the foothills to the distant lights of the cities of the valley. They glowed like distant galaxies, hanging as unsupported as I in the cold emptiness of night. I could rotate, and it seemed as if the whole dark world and a billion stars were turning around me. Here and there, at some unimaginable distance, a spark moved: a car on a highway, a plane.

Too soon, it was past midnight. I was cold and tired; with my hands in my pockets, I headed for home.

Just for a smile, I buzzed the air base control tower, coming down to within five hundred feet of it at a speed of over a hundred miles per hour. It made my eyes water like crazy, but it was fun. A few seconds later I slipped between the branches of the willow tree and into my room. A few seconds after that, a jet fighter boomed past overhead. I undressed, giggling quietly to myself in the darkness.

The War To Stamp Out Amnesic Male Idiots was still raging the next morning. I intercepted Pat on her way to school, but she wouldn't even talk to me, let alone get in the car. Finally I parked Brunhilde in somebody's driveway, right across her path, and got out.

"Look, this is crazy," I said. "I'm really sorry I forgot to pick you up yesterday, okay? I've been feeling really stupid about it—"

"Good." She gave me a magnum-force dirty look and limped across somebody's flowerbed to get around me.

I reached out to grab her hand. "Pat, please—"

She swung her cane across my forearm like a cavalry saber and I yelped, stumbling back against the car.

"Stay clear of me. Just stay clear of me."

I stood there, watching her go on down the sidewalk, while I rubbed my arm. That was some whack she'd given me; I felt a belated twinge of sympathy for Jason Murphy's shin.

The garage door started rising at the end of somebody's driveway, and somebody himself came rolling out in his red BMW. He saw me and Brunhilde blocking his driveway and stuck his head out the window.

"Hey, you wanna move it, buddy?"

Always willing to oblige, I got in and backed out. Then I gunned the motor and took off. Old VWs are very poor for making dramatic exits in; they don't leave rubber or roar a lot, they just wheeze louder. I passed Pat, who didn't look at me. She didn't seem so mad now, just unhappy. If I hadn't been so sore at her, I'd have stopped and tried again. But I *was* sore, and my arm hurt, and I had that grainy-eyeball, half-zonked feeling of being without enough sleep, so I went on past.

Bobby Gassaway was practically frothing in the lab. His

dad had taken a couple of Polaroid snaps of last night's UFO on the radar screen; they looked like nothing in particular, but Bobby seemed to think they were the hottest evidence this side of an outright invasion from space.

Gibbs was less impressed. "These are interesting, Gassaway," he said, "but they certainly don't prove anything except that an unknown aircraft was overhead last night."

"But, Mr. Gibbs, my dad says it couldn't have been an aircraft. The radar profile was all wrong. It hardly turned up at all, just like the last couple of times. Whatever it was, it was little and made out of something that hardly reflects radar at all, so right there we can forget about human technology. And it came right down toward the control tower just before it disappeared."

"Gassaway, you're trying to have it both ways. Has anybody *seen* anything?"

"I don't think so, sir. At least not the controllers."

"So your only evidence is a blip on a screen, and not even a very strong blip. For all you know, it could be some prankster with a radio-controlled model airplane, or an owl."

"Sir." Gassaway was all wounded dignity. "My dad knows what he sees on radar, and he says he's never seen anything like this."

"And yet you started this project on the grounds that he sees UFOs all the time."

"Well, he *does*, Mr. Gibbs. But this one just happens to be different. I'll tell you this—they took it seriously enough to scramble a jet."

Gibbs regarded Gassaway dispassionately. "And did the jet pilot see anything?"

"No, sir. It vanished again."

"What's the principle of Occam's razor, Gassaway?"

"Well—that you should always choose the simplest explanation that fits the facts, sir."

"Good. What do you consider the simplest explanation for these radar sightings?"

"I lean to some kind of small, unmanned craft from a mother ship, sir."

Gibbs kept his face immobile. "Why not a small, unmanned model airplane?"

"Because one of the facts is that my father is a qualified air traffic controller and he eliminated that possibility, sir."

"You don't think it could be the work of some prankster?"

"Sir, now *you* better get out Occam's razor. It's hard to imagine how a prankster could handle something so small, but that can climb up to eighteen thousand feet in next to no time, or travel just a couple of hundred feet up at almost a hundred miles an hour."

"Gassaway, you're making some dubious assumptions."

"I don't think so, sir."

"How do you know that whatever climbed to eighteen thousand feet the other night is the same thing your father saw on radar last night?"

"Well, sir, it's just been the last few days that he's seen this kind of image."

"Gassaway, what does *post hoc ergo propter hoc* mean?"

"It's a fallacy, Mr. Gibbs. It means, 'after this, therefore because of this.' And I see where you're getting. Just because they've seen something funny a couple of nights running doesn't mean it's the same thing. But I could just as easily argue that just because you look like the teacher we saw yesterday doesn't mean you *are* Mr. Gibbs. You could be an impostor."

"What conclusions would follow from that hypothesis?" Gibbs asked, not at all put out.

"Uh, well, that some kind of conspiracy was under way?"

"What kind of conspiracy would require the replacement of a high-school science teacher?"

"Maybe somebody doesn't want the truth about UFOs to come out."

"Or maybe San Cristobal is getting serious about beating us tomorrow," Gibbs answered with a smile. Most of us laughed.

"Aw, come on, Mr. Gibbs. Why would they do that?"

"Give me some time and I can cook up any story you like. Gassaway, the point is this: a theory doesn't just explain things. It *dis*explains things, too. If it asks us to throw away too much of what we think we already know, we've got a right to ask for iron-clad proof. That's why Galileo and Darwin bothered people. Their theories threatened some very detailed and satisfactory bodies of knowledge. Now, maybe these

UFOs of yours do exist. But if they do, their existence means some great big chunks of science are very wrong, and we'll have to go back and do a whole lot of work from scratch. Nobody wants to do that until the evidence is incontrovertible —and until the new theory makes some predictions that can be tested."

"Well, sir, I think the evidence is incontrovertible that something is out there."

"Occam's razor tells me it's a hoaxer or a misinterpreted natural phenomenon, Gassaway."

I raised my hand. "Mr. Gibbs, I think the evidence points to a hoaxer. Somebody who's found a way to fool the air force radar. Bobby, when have these UFOs been turning up?"

Gassaway turned a look of deadly suspicion on me. "Between about 11:00 P.M. and midnight, sometimes a little later. Why?"

"Well, I'll predict that another one turns up tonight around that time."

"Stevenson, are you pulling something on me?" Gassaway's face was pale. "Because if you are, so help me—"

"Bobby, I'm telling you the absolute truth when I say I'm not a hoaxer. Okay? I wouldn't know how to fool a radar beam if my life depended on it. But it seems logical that if somebody has figured out a way to do it, they'll keep doing it—especially if now the air force is reacting by sending up jets. So I'll predict that they'll do it again tonight, probably about the same time."

"Your prediction doesn't necessarily validate the hoaxer theory, Stevenson," said Gibbs. "Sunrise is another periodic phenomenon, but no one supposes that it's due to a hoaxer."

"Maybe not, sir, but if Gassaway is really looking sharp tonight, and so is the air force, they might be able to spot this UFO and identify it once and for all."

Gibbs nodded absently. "Well, Gassaway can try to test your theory tonight."

All through this exchange I'd been glancing over at Pat, trying to see if she was paying any attention. She wasn't.

The rest of the day dragged along. After school, practice was almost like a regular game: the bleachers were jammed and people stood around the sidelines. Cheerleaders were doing their routines and getting a big reaction. The weedy young guy with the tape recorder was there again, along with a camera crew from the local TV station. Gibbs ignored it all and barked like an alpha-male baboon dealing with the dumbest young apes in his troop. We barked back and ran around trying to look fierce. I did my thing, mostly with running, and the crowd ate it up. At the end of practice the TV crew wanted to interview me, but Gibbs vetoed it. I showered and headed for home.

I was *bushed*. I'd had maybe six hours' sleep for two nights in a row; I'd run around trying to avoid being tackled by large psychopaths, and hadn't always succeeded; and I'd evidently broken up with the first girl I'd ever really cared about. When I thought about last weekend, up in the hills, I couldn't believe it had been real.

So I shuffled into the house and headed upstairs, hoping to grab a nap before dinner. Melinda called from the kitchen, and I trudged back down.

Some kind of casserole was cooking in the oven, and Melinda had made a big salad. She was sitting at the kitchen table with the newspaper and a glass of white wine.

"Hi. Sit and have a Coke or something."

I had a tonic water.

"There's a story about you in the paper tonight."

"Yeah? I'm gonna be on TV, too."

She smiled, but a little distantly. "Quite a change, isn't it? Being a big jock?"

"I guess. I don't know why everyone makes such a fuss. It's a lot like being involved in a mass mugging."

"And the prize for the most insincere display of modesty goes to—Rick Stevenson! Win it one more time and we'll retire the cup."

"Aw, come on, Melinda. I hardly know what the heck I'm doing out there. Everybody else knows plays and strategy; they just tell me what to do and they give me the ball and I run."

"Boloney. You're fantastic out there."

"You really believe what you read in the papers?"

"The papers say you're phenomenal, not fantastic. I've been to your practices the last two days."

"Huh? And you didn't tell me?"

"I just did. Don't get sore, Rick. I just thought you didn't need to get all self-conscious."

"Boy. Start playing football and everybody goes weird on you. Willy practically fires me. You sneak around to watch me. And Pat won't even talk to me."

"Why not?"

I yawned, shaking my head. *"I* don't know. She got sore because I couldn't see her on Monday night, and then one thing just led to another. I even overslept and forgot to pick her up, and apologizing doesn't do any good."

Melinda looked at me with those big intelligent blue eyes of hers. "What do you think about her, Rick?"

"I *think* she's a pain in the ass. I *feel* she's the only girl I've ever met who's worth caring about."

"I bet she feels just the same way about you. You're a smart cookie, and you can be cute sometimes, but you're a real ego-flexer and you're not always so hot at handling other people's feelings."

Usually I would roll my eyes and come up with a snappy retort when Melinda gave me this poor-repressed-macho-cripple routine. This time I was too tired and dull, so instead I said: "What have I been doing wrong?"

"You've been closing yourself off, Rick. You started opening up a little after that damn computer got taken away, and you opened up to Pat. You made her start to think she could relax and trust you. Then you just—relapsed. Went off the air. All week long—hell, it's been longer than that, really, but this week it's been really bad. I don't know why you're doing it, but from out here it looks like you want to break up with Pat but you don't have the guts to say so."

"Why would I want to do that?"

She looked at me in a way I'd never seen before—as if she were looking at somebody else, somebody she didn't like at all.

"Beats the hell out of me, Rick. It just looks like you've got something else to interest you—or somebody else." She poured herself another glass and I realized she'd been efficiently putting away most of the bottle while we talked. Very un-Melinda.

"If you really want to know, you remind me a lot of your father just lately."

Do you ever get the funny feeling that the person you're talking to is suddenly very far away, and then very close? That was the feeling I got then. Melinda's face seemed to retreat and advance.

"How so?" I asked, trying to sound casual. On the few occasions when I'd asked her about him before, she'd given me short, angry answers.

"He was really, really good at all kinds of things. Especially at closing himself off in his own little world. It was—" She shook her head, and I saw tears gleam in her eyes. "He was such a bright, funny guy, but he couldn't face responsibility. He couldn't face being alone, either. So he'd try to reassure himself by attracting some girl, and then, as soon as she was hooked, he'd walk away. Just leave her there. 'Babe, it's not working out,' he'd say in that deep voice of his. 'I guess I'm not really your kind of guy. I'm just big trouble for you.' And . . . off he'd go."

I felt paralyzed. I wanted to tell Melinda that I wasn't like that, that I had a real reason for behaving the way I was. But I didn't want to argue with her because she might get off the subject of my father and it could be years before she felt like mentioning him again.

"Is that what he did with you?"

"Word for word. Oh, he said a lot more. But he managed to get it all said in about twenty minutes, and then he kissed me and walked out the door. I was almost three months pregnant."

"And he walked out on you anyway?"

"He didn't know, and I sure wasn't going to tell him."

"But why not? My gosh, he—"

"If I couldn't hold on to him by myself, I sure as hell wasn't going to use *you* to do it. I didn't want him living with me under duress, being the dutiful husband and father, and sneaking off to reassure himself with a string of new girlfriends."

"Did you ever hear from him again?"

"I made sure I couldn't. I moved out of town, quit school, came out to California and had you. Then I went back to school and—here we are."

"Where'd you been living?"

"Maybe I'll tell you when you're eighteen or twenty-one or whatever age you have to be to be grown up these days." She finished the bottle. "I know you've got a right to know who your father was and all that. I just don't feel like seeing him again, and I'd probably have to if you got back in touch with him. So if it's all the same to you, I'd just as soon not talk about him anymore."

"He must have been some guy," I said.

"Some jerk is more like it."

"Yeah, maybe. But he attracted you, and he spoiled you for anybody else."

Melinda looked steadily at me, not quite focused properly, and smiled wistfully. "Yeah, he attracted me, all right, and I guess he did spoil me. Everybody else was boring by comparison. And I did some comparing, believe me."

"Melinda? Are you ever sorry you didn't try to get back with him?"

"Oh, sometimes. Most of the time I'm just sore that he had to be such a schmuck, and glad I didn't end up living with him so long I got tired of him." She wiped her eyes and stood up. "Dinner."

It was a good casserole, full of beef and noodles and mushrooms, and the salad was even better—spinach and hard-boiled eggs and radishes and tomatoes, with one of those dressings Melinda makes up. We sat and ate and talked about football and architecture and computers. I talked a lot, but I wasn't listening to myself very much. Instead, I sat back inside my head and debated with myself about other things. After dinner, we ate canned peaches and ice cream while the debate continued. Melinda went back to work in her study while I did the dishes under Marcus's supervision. The phone rang just as I was finishing up, and Melinda picked it up in the study.

"It's for you. Jerry Ames."

Wiping my hands on a dishtowel, I went into the study and took the phone.

"Yo, Rick Doin' anything?"

"Nothing much at the moment."

"Feel like cruising Santa Barbara Boulevard? Kind of a good way to relax before a game."

I was too surprised to say anything for a moment. "I don't know, Jerry."

"C'mon, it'll do you good. We'll pick up a couple of girls, have a good time, get ourselves relaxed."

"Uh, I think I better take a rain check on this one, Jerry. I have to see Pat tonight."

"Ah, hey, I didn't know that was still alive, y'know?"

Melinda, sitting in front of her computer, was giving me a big, smug, maternal grin. I could've slugged her with the phone.

"Well, you know," I said wittily.

"Yeah. Well, okay, maybe we'll do something this week-end, unwind, y'know?"

"Yeah, maybe so. Take care of that arm."

"Take care of those legs, man."

I hung up and Melinda bellowed, *"Yay!* You're really going to go see Pat?"

"Well, I'm going to try. If she mails me back here in six small boxes, it's all your fault. Okay if I bring her back?"

"Sure! Why not? Go on, call her."

"Uh, I think I've got a better chance if I just show up."

"Do it your way. Just don't fumble the ball."

"Would you quit it with the sports metaphors?" I begged. "See you later."

I went out and got into Brunhilde while fantasizing that this was the Battle of Britain and I was climbing into my Spitfire. Maybe I'd come home in glory, and maybe I'd go down in flames.

Pat's place was relatively quiet; my sternum didn't start vibrating to the stereo until I was actually on the front porch. After some aerobic knocking, I finally got a sign of life: one of the other girls, a sallow little kid with a handful of eye shadow on each lid answered the door. Her name was Lauri; she was Pat's roommate.

"Hi," I said. Joe Cool. "Pat in?"

"I dunno. Wanna go see?"

"Might as well."

Inside, the stereo crashed and banged while three girls sat squabbling in the living room about whose turn it was to help Morty and Joan with breakfast tomorrow. They glanced up at me and went back to their squabble. Morty popped in from the kitchen.

"*Please* turn down the music, girls. Oh, hi, Rick. Didn't expect to see you tonight. Shall I call Pat downstairs?"

"Uh, maybe it would be easier if I just went up and knocked on her door. My mother and I wanted to invite her over for the evening."

"Well, go on up. Maybe she can use a night out. She hasn't been the greatest company the last few days."

Oh boy. I went upstairs and down the hall to the room that Pat shared with the Eyeshadow Queen, and knocked.

"Go away."

I nearly did. The thought of going back empty-handed to Melinda was all that kept me from doing an about-face and retreating.

Instead, I opened the door. Pat was sitting at her desk, doing calculus and wearing her usual at-home outfit: jeans, UCLA sweatshirt, and ear plugs. Her face hardened when she saw me.

Moving fast, I crossed the room and sat down on the bed next to her desk.

"I've got to talk to you."

"I've got nothing to say to you."

"You don't have to say anything if you don't want to. Come back to our place for a little while. Melinda would love to see you, and if you're still mad at me when I've explained things, I won't bother you anymore."

I could see her emotions battling each other. For a while it looked likely that she was going to bash me with her calculus textbook and leave me for dead.

"Okay," she said finally. "Let's go."

We drove back through the chilly evening, not saying much and listening to a Bach tape. When we got home, Melinda was still at work but came out of the study to give Pat a big hello and offer her a cup of tea. We sat drinking and eating cookies in the kitchen for a few minutes, while Pat and

Melinda nattered about nothing in particular. Finally Melinda said she had to go back to work.

"Come on upstairs," I said. "I can't show you what this is all about down here."

Pat gave me a dubious look, but decided I wasn't likely to do anything too violent. So we went upstairs, with her taking each step slowly and carefully just like the old days of a week before. Marcus came with us and flopped down on the carpet with his usual grunt. Pat settled into the chair by my work-bench.

"So what is this famous new experiment?" she asked coolly. "Some new EEG?"

"No. I just want you to watch something. Please don't make a fuss, okay? I don't want to upset Melinda or anything. She doesn't know anything about it. And I have to ask you to keep it a secret."

"Sure, but it better be good."

I sat crosslegged on my bed and took a deep breath. Believe it or not, I felt a little shaky, as if I was about to take off my clothes in public or something equally weird. "I learned I could do this a few weeks ago—in fact, it was the day you started school."

And I lifted about a foot off the bed, with my hands on my knees. Marcus glanced at me and went to sleep. Pat watched without a change in her expression. Then one hand rose slowly to cover her mouth, and her eyes began to widen.

Without saying anything else, I rotated clockwise through 360 degrees. Then I tipped forward and did a kind of slow-motion somersault in place. I moved sideways toward the window, and then back toward the door. Pat didn't move.

"Can I come a little closer to you?" I asked quietly.

She nodded, very slowly. With my legs still crossed, I moved across the room until I was close enough to touch her.

"I'm still learning how to do it," I explained. "That's why I didn't invite you over, because I was practicing. I guess it's what they call levitation, but I just call it lifting."

She reached up, taking my hands in hers, and she was smiling.

"You look beautiful up there. Teach me how to do it, too."

9

THE BIOFEEDBACK DEVICE and the EEG had been gathering dust on my workbench all week. With slightly shaky hands, I set them up beside the bed. The only way I could fight the urge to babble was to keep my trap shut. After all these weeks, the desire to share everything was, in itself, nearly strong enough lift me off the floor.

Pat must have wanted to talk, too, but she took her cue from me: if silence was part of the drill, she'd be silent. I sat her down on the edge of the bed and taped the electrodes to her temples and scalp. Paste would've made a better connection, but it was getting late and she didn't need to explain to Morty why she had this weird guck in her hair.

"Okay," I said at last. "You can sit or lie down, whatever feels comfortable. Relax as much as you can. When the light goes on, try to keep it on. It may be hard, because you'll feel kind of sleepy and when you concentrate you start waking yourself up."

"I'm an old pro at this now." She heaved her bad leg onto the bed, swung the good one up beside it, and stretched out. "I feel like the Bride of Frankenstein."

She shouldn't have said that, because it set me off on the worst attack of giggles I'd had in years. And that set her off, too, so nothing much happened except the gadgets consumed electricity. After a while we calmed down, and talked quietly about nothing much; as if by agreement, we didn't talk about lifting.

The light went on and off erratically, and then began going on for longer periods. Pat's face softened; she didn't look tired, just relaxed in a way I'd never seen her before. Sitting a few feet away, I watched her with growing surprise. She was more beautiful than ever, but that wasn't what surprised me: I knew I was looking at the real Pat, the girl I'd intuitively known was trapped under the anger and hurt and loneliness. This was a girl who was utterly open and yet unknowable, mysterious; her faint smile made her seem both young and ageless.

"I love you," I said quietly.

"I love you, too," she murmured. She didn't look up, or change her expression; her sleepy eyes were focused on the light, keeping it on.

"I want you to try to feel something. It's like being in a Jacuzzi, a kind of moving, tingly pressure all over your body."

". . . No. I don't feel anything like that."

"Like something strong and fast, moving over your skin?"

"No . . ."

She lay there for almost half an hour; the light began to go off, flickering uncertainly.

"I can't feel it, Rick," she whispered.

I pulled my chair closer and took her hand. "Just keep the light on. You'll feel it." And I turned on the Effect, not enough to lift but enough to make myself aware of the endless pulsing energy all around me. Pat's eyes widened a little, then closed.

"Oh—I feel *that*. Feels good." I could see the fine gold hairs on her arms stand up. "It *is* like a Jacuzzi."

"Can you feel it all over you?"

"Mm-hm."

"Make it stronger underneath you." I was still holding her hand, and I lifted about an inch.

So did Pat.

I held my breath, lifting ever so gently higher: two inches, three, four. The electrode cables began to tighten. Pat looked at me, her eyes half-closed, a faint smile still on her lips.

"You're lifting," I told her.

"I know."

The light flickered and went out, but Pat stayed up. I reached over with my other hand and, as gently as I could, I pulled the electrodes off.

"I feel it, Rick. I really, really feel it." She let go of my hand. Then she drifted up to within a foot of the ceiling. Slowly she circled the room, still horizontal, her fingers occasionally touching the ceiling. "It feels so strange, but so—ordinary. Natural, like I've always been able to do it."

"I know." And I lifted up to float beside her, put my arms around her, and kissed her.

Half an hour later, we were driving back to her place.

"It's got to stay a secret, at least for a while," I said.

"I know. But, oh God, I can't believe it's really happened. A couple of hours ago I was doing my homework, and now I can fly." Just to prove it, she lifted off her seat and bumped her head.

I laughed. "Quit that! Listen. This weekend I want to take you back up in the hills, where nobody can see us, so we can practice some real flying. And I'll finally be able to tell you what's been going on."

"You stinker, I can guess a lot of it already. That's how you got me off the hillside, isn't it? Uh-huh. And why you built the EEG in the first place."

"The first time, I did it with nothing," I bragged. "The EEG was just to get me back in the mood."

"In the mood. I'll never be *out* of the mood. It's—oh, Rick, this is a miracle."

"Don't let Gibbs hear you talking that way."

"Hey, let's blow his mind tomorrow, come in through the windows."

"Don't even *talk* about it. We'll show it to him, but not just yet. I want to get a better idea of what the Effect is, what we can do with it. And I want to make sure we don't get hurt when we do go public."

She nodded, a little sobered. "I don't want to be famous. I just want to lift all the time."

"Don't we all. But for now we've got to do a real Clark Kent number, secret identities, all that good stuff."

"You mean I get to wear a mask and a leotard?"

"No, just a mask."

"Anything you say. You're the boss—on this."

"Boss, shmoss. I just don't want us getting shot or put in some lab." We pulled up in front of her house. "Uh, can I assume you're coming to the game tomorrow?"

"Sure, if you promise to take me out after."

"I promise."

I walked her to the door. Morty had seen us arrive, and had the door open.

"Hi, Mort!" she chirped.

"Hi, Pat. How are you?"

"Just fine! See you tomorrow morning, Rick?"

"Pick you up about eight?"

"Great. G'night." And she limped off inside. Morty glanced over his shoulder at her, then turned back to me.

"Gee—she sure must've needed a night out. Nice to have her so cheerful for a change. Night, Rick. Thanks."

Friday morning, Pat was waiting out on the sidewalk. It was a crisp, clear morning, with dew on the grass and the promise of frost before long. Pat was wearing a blue duffel coat and jeans, with her books in a backpack. She swung into the car and kissed me hard enough to dent my face.

"I could hardly sleep last night," she said as I started the car. "I kept lifting."

"What about your roommate, the eyeshadow monster?"

"Lauri? She snored all night. Besides, I was just lifting myself up off the bed a little—just an inch or two. I can't get over it, Rick. It's just the greatest feeling in the world—happy and scary all together. Are you sure this isn't a dream?"

"I doubt it. Melinda would never let me sleep for a month and a half." I squeezed her hand. "It feels good to have someone else to share it with."

"Mr. Stevenson, I'll tell you this. When you have a secret, it's a doozy. I can hardly wait for your next revelation."

"The next revelation is that San Cristobal is going to be

massacred tonight," I predicted modestly.

"I can't wait. Can I play, too?"

"You get your turn after the game."

"Rick—are we really going outside, up in the air?"

"What's the point of lifting just inside a room, when the whole world is out there? It's a great feeling."

"How high are we going?"

"A few hundred feet. You have to remember to wear dark clothes."

"Don't worry."

"And I'll get you a balaclava to cover your face. It makes you look like Spiderman, but it keeps your face warm and covers it up."

"Fine. And are we really going hiking tomorrow?"

"Why not? You got something better to do?"

"Uh-uh."

Jason Murphy's white Trans Am swam up behind us in my rearview mirror. He tailgated me for a minute, then swung out and passed with a roar. One of the Tricycle Rats, sitting beside him, gave us the finger.

I sighed. "Some people have no respect for superheroes."

Gassaway was lurking in the lab, and when we came in he pounced on me.

"The great prophet!" he crowed. "The Nostradamus of Santa Teresa! The famous UFO predictor."

My jaw dropped. "I f—" Just in time, I caught myself from saying I'd forgotten all about my predicted UFO, and gone straight to bed last night. "What d'you mean?" I asked coolly.

"No UFOs! Not a trace! And you predicted one."

"Yeah." I shrugged like a good loser. "Well, can't win 'em all."

"Ye of little faith." Gassaway grinned. It wasn't a pretty sight.

"Maybe you'll get lucky tonight," I suggested.

"Want to make that a prediction?"

"Not this time. But keep your eyes peeled. One of these nights you might even see the Great Pumpkin."

Actually, I felt embarrassed. Here I'd started to set up a great practical joke on Gassaway and the whole U.S. Air

Force, and then it had slipped my mind. Maybe too much lifting could induce amnesia? No, it was just my usual absent-mindedness.

Pat and I sat together, which interested Gibbs not at all but caused Angela to go into spasms of curiosity until Pat finally got a chance to tell her that all was well. She looked a little disappointed; I think she'd been enjoying despising me. The rest of the Awkward Squad was agog about our reconciliation for all of fifteen seconds, which was about its maximum attention span.

The morning went along smoothly; Gibbs did a great job of teaching and I did a great job of fretting about the game. Finally I had to go to the john. Jason and a couple of the Tricycle Rats were there, conducting a tobacco seminar, and they cheered up when they saw me.

"The mutant!" Jason exclaimed. "Faster than a speeding bullet. Able to leap tall buildings."

I finished what I was doing and went to wash my hands. If I'd had any sense, I would've ignored him and left. Instead, I said: "Jason, what's your problem?"

"Man, I don't have any problems. I get along pretty good. But I got, y'know, standards. Like, a code? The code says you don't have to put up with jerks who think they're cool, y'know? 'Cause that's dishonest, it's like lying if you're a jerk and you try to cover it up. You're a jerk, you should act like a jerk."

"Hey, right on," said one of the Tricycle Rats. I could never tell them apart, and I wasn't about to start trying now.

"Well, it's good to see somebody who actually practices what they preach," I said.

"Huh?" said Jason.

"Never mind."

"Well, so everybody thinks you're some kind of a hot foot-ball player all of a sudden. But we know you're still a jerk."

"Yeah, but so what?" I asked. "I mean, with all the prob-lems in the world, why should you worry about me?"

"For one thing, because you think you're a lot smarter than you really are. For another thing, because you got no class. And for another thing, you blindsided me in that game."

"Oh, boloney," I said, and the next thing I knew I was

staggering back into the wall with the right side of my face ringing like a gong. Jason had slugged me and I hadn't even seen it coming.

"You—you know, you're a classic sociopath," I gasped.

Classic sociopaths are never impressed by that kind of talk. The Tricycle Rats grabbed my arms while Jason drew back for another punch. I turned on the Effect, but not fast enough to avoid a sock in the stomach. Then I used the Effect to whirl me and the Rats counterclockwise. That swung the guy on my left arm right into the wall, and sent the other one crashing into Jason, who swore as the two of them fell backward into the urinals. Jason Murphy with his skinny backside wedged into the bottom of a urinal was a very cheering sight. I feasted my eyes for a moment, thought about getting off a good parting shot, and then decided to just get out while the getting was good.

Pat's antennae picked up my adrenaline aura as soon as I came back into the lab.

"What's the matter?"

"Just got punched out by Jason in the can," I said a little thickly. The inside of my cheek was a little ragged, and my jaw hurt.

"What? *Why?*"

"He got a chance."

"Well, that sucker has gone far enough. Let's turn him in."

"Forget it. Living well is the best revenge."

"My idea of living well is to put Jason's head in a Cuisinart."

"For*get* it," I insisted. "I'm already all knotted up about the game. I don't need anything else right now."

"But—"

"Look, you're batting a thousand against Jason so far, but I'm not, and I don't want to. He's just a distraction."

She subsided, thanks more to a glower from Gibbs than to my own irrefutable logic, and the subject was dropped.

The day went on, getting steadily giddier. Lunch was a mob scene, with the team and the fans all hanging around, and I found it really hard to pay attention to my afternoon classes —partly because I was nervous and partly because my jaw hurt like mad. After school I brought Pat home; Melinda made an early dinner and we had a good time cracking jokes and making bets on how long I'd survive. Then we left for the game.

The school looked different in the early evening, with the floodlights blazing down on crowded stands. I hate to admit it, but this was the first Terry High football game I'd ever attended, and I was observing everything with a kind of anthropological interest. The mood in the locker room was a lot different from the afternoon practices; guys were talking more loudly than usual, laughing more abruptly. I got my shoulder punched a lot.

Finally we were all dressed up and ready to go. Gibbs had been standing around, not saying much, but now he took up a position by the door to the corridor that led out to the field. He was looking sharp in blue slacks and his blue-and-gold coach's Windbreaker, and his expression was grim.

"This game is a test," he said after a long pause. "It's a test of how well we can come back after losing Powell. It's a test of how well we can adapt our plays to Stevenson, and how well he can adapt to a game he's not familiar with."

He was putting on enough pressure to pop my eardrums; everybody looked at me.

"We are up against one of the best teams in the state," Gibbs went on. "They are tough, they are smart, and they are quick. They always come to play. They've heard about Stevenson, and they are going to test him and try to shake him up. Our job will be to give them so much else to think about, they may not even notice Stevenson until he's in the end zone.

"This is a physical team we're playing against tonight. They like to hit hard. We are going to have to hit harder, or they will take our own field away from us. Will we let them do that?"

"*No*, sir!"

"Damn right we won't. We're going out there and scare them sick."

"*Yes*, sir!"

"We're going to make those people out there realize that they have seen the game of the year, a game we've won."

"*Yes*, sir!"

"What are you waiting for?"

With a rumble and a clatter, we took off past him, down the corridor and out onto the field. The crowd was cheering, the band was playing, and I thought it was all silly but fun. We did our warm-up exercises and got ready for the kickoff.

Gibbs kept me out of the game for the first quarter. He sat next to me on the bench, analyzing San Cristobal's strategy and pointing out the players I'd have to watch out for. It was helpful, but also demoralizing: I could barely follow what was going on, while Gibbs sat with his legs crossed and his hands in his Windbreaker pockets, predicting what San Cristobal would do before they even came out of their huddle. Then they'd do it, as if he'd devised their plays. In the melee of thrashing bodies out on the field, Gibbs could pick out a single player and discuss the guy's performance in detail—while I was still trying to find the guy.

When I finally went in, early in the second quarter, we were down 7–0. Gibbs didn't seem to care; in contrast to the way he screamed at us in training sessions, he was calm and quiet. He let Jerry Ames decide on the plays, and the only message he sent with me onto the field was to keep up the good work.

I'm not going to bore you with a yard-by-yard account of my noble exploits. In the second quarter I scored twice, within five minutes, and Gibbs pulled me off again before San Cristobal could figure out what had hit them. The crowd was noisy; I ignored it until a piercing whistle rang out. I recognized it as Melinda's, and glanced over my shoulder. She and Pat were in the fourth or fifth row, directly behind the bench, and having a disgustingly good time.

At half time I went back to the locker room with the team, expecting Gibbs to praise us to the skies. Instead, he sandblasted our egos with a detailed description of our technical errors, physical inadequacies, and moral lapses—including mine, and he didn't make allowances for my neophyte status.

"Now, people, our visitors are considering what to do in the next quarter, and I expect they'll decide to get physical and try to scare us into making even more mistakes. They'll be waiting for Stevenson especially, and try to take him out or scare him."

Whoopee, I thought.

"So we're going to teach them very quickly that it won't work. Stevenson, remember how you took out Quackenbush the other day?"

"Yes, sir." So did Sean; he had bruises all over his rib cage.

"Right away, on our first play, I want you to take out that big tackle of theirs, that Al Suarez. I don't care if you don't make any yardage, so long as he learns to treat you with respect."

"Yes, sir, " I repeated dully. Colliding with Sean had been a lot like jumping face-first into a wall. Suarez was even bigger than Sean.

"You don't sound all that eager, Stevenson, and I don't blame you. But if you don't, those people are going to treat you like a trampoline. They don't want to see you score any more touchdowns."

"Okay, Mr. Gibbs."

"Good." Having rubbed our noses in our failings, he now began to build us up again, praising Jerry's quarterbacking, Sean's tackling, saying something good about each of us and holding out the glorious opportunity of a whole new half awaiting us.

It was a great performance; even while part of me was marvelling at what a master manipulator Gibbs was, the rest of me was overdosing on adrenaline and slavering to get back into action.

On our first play in the third quarter, Jerry did as Gibbs had ordered: handed me the ball as I took off around right end. I was getting up a lot of speed, and if I'd wanted to I probably could have outrun Suarez without looking *too* fast. But I saw him coming and let him intercept just as I piled on some more Effect.

Thud.

I hit him with my shoulder, hip, and knee virturally simultaneously, so hard the football nearly popped away from me. Suarez said *"Huhhhh!"* and spun away before he toppled. I could hardly breathe, but I was still on my feet with a little momentum, so I kept going. Touchdown number three.

As with Jason, I trotted back to see my opponent on the ground. But his coach was kneeling beside him, and another coach was opening a little satchel next to Suarez.

Sean Quackenbush slapped my backside as I passed him.
"Way to go, Stevenson! Geez, you really thumped him a good
one. I kind of sympathize with the poor guy."

I couldn't even see Suarez now because of all the players
and coaches circled around him. Time-out had been called;
after a few minutes, a couple of kids scuttled out onto the field
with a stretcher. Suarez went off on it to a burst of applause.

I saw some of the San Cristobal players looking at me
thoughtfully as we carried on with the game. The next time I
carried the ball, they came at me low, trying to grab my legs. I
lifted over them. Touchdown number four. The Terry High
fans were jumping up and down, the band was playing the
theme from *Rocky* (which nearly made me sick), and Mr.
Gordon was grinning away up in the stands.

The next time I was off the field, I could hardly hear Gibbs
because of all the uproar in the stands behind us. He told me
to keep it up, and not to be afraid of hitting anybody else who
got in my way.

"Is Suarez okay?" I shouted in his ear.

"I expect. He's built to take it."

San Cristobal came back pretty strongly about then, and
scored another touchdown that was elegant even to my amateur eye. They were playing wide-open ball now, taking
chances and exploiting opportunities they knew might never
come again. By the end of the third quarter, the score was
28–14 and San Cristobal definitely had momentum. Early in
the fourth quarter they scored yet again. Gibbs turned to me.

"Get in there and do your thing, Stevenson. Don't be afraid
of them."

So I did, and I wasn't. Jerry Ames handed me the ball and
I took off, outrunning my own blockers in a few steps.
Nobody on the other team even got close, and we made the
conversion just as the quarter ended. The score was 35–14.

As we were getting reorganized for the fourth quarter, San
Cristobal's coach sent in a substitute who went from player to
player, speaking briefly to each one. I came off the field at
that point.

"You're doing very well, Stevenson," Gibbs said. "That
should about do it. They did their best and it wasn't good

enough. They'll start to come apart in this quarter."

Instead, the guys from San Cristobal went berserk.

In less than five minutes they scored a touchdown, made the conversion, and sacked Jerry Ames right out of the game. Gibbs sent in Mike Palmer, and they sacked him, too, but not as badly. Then they scored another touchdown, and the score was 35–28. We were suddenly very much on the defensive.

Jerry Ames, sitting on the bench with his ankle puffing up, explained what was going on.

"They heard that guy of theirs, Suarez, is in real bad shape. Couple of broken ribs, maybe some internal injuries. They took him to the hospital. So the team's kinda browned off."

Gibbs didn't say anything, and neither did I. But I felt odd. I hadn't meant to put the guy in hospital.

We were playing badly now; the team obviously missed Jerry, and Mike was a good guy but they'd rattled him on that sack. When San Cristobal got the ball again, they marched downfield with it, shoving us out of the way or going right over us. At this rate they were going to tie it up, and after the pasting they'd taken, that would be as good as a victory for them.

"Get back in there," Gibbs ordered me. "We need somebody fast out there to catch their runners."

The San Cristobal fans started booing when I came out, which made me feel uncomfortable. Their team watched me trot out with cold expressions on their faces. I had a feeling they wouldn't mind losing the game if they could stomp me flat in the next few minutes.

I hadn't had much experience playing defense, and on the first couple of plays I didn't have much to do. Then San Cristobal's quarterback popped a soft, low pass right over my head; I didn't even have to lift to intercept it, and I can see now that they wanted me to.

With the ball under my arm I took off, but one of their players grabbed me by the leg just as about three others piled on. I hit the ground and an instant later felt a blinding pain in my back; one of them had kneed me in the kidneys.

"That's for Big Al, buddy," the guy hissed in my ear. "And it's just for starters."

I lurched to my feet, barely able to stand upright. A dull

growl came from the monster in my basement. It was one thing to hurt a guy unintentionally, but something else again to go gunning for somebody. This morning I'd been punched in the face by one jerk, and now some two-hundred-pound clown had nearly broken my back. Who needed this?

In the huddle, I asked Mike Palmer to try a quick, short pass to me once I got past the line of scrimmage. He agreed; after five touchdowns, I was pretty popular.

On the play, Mike faked a hand-off and then dropped back while I shot around left end. The pass was beautiful, fast and accurate, and I looked it into my hands the way Gibbs had taught me.

Meanwhile, San Cristobal's whole backfield was converging on me. I pivoted away from one guy and accelerated toward another—the character who'd kneed me. We collided hard, harder than he was ready for, and ricocheted apart. I saw him lose his balance; then I was away, with the crowd roaring and the band playing.

At that point the fight really did go out of San Cristobal. The guy who'd kneed me was writhing on the grass, clutching his leg. The others stood around looking at me in a different way, and I realized that they were actually scared of me—me, the famous athletic shnook.

It was all going on like a silent movie, because the crowd was yelling on one side and booing on the other, and it was almost impossible to hear what people on the field were saying. We watched San Cristobal's latest casualty go off the field between two other players, his bunged-up leg lifted just enough to keep weight off it. His coach met him on the sideline and gave him a sympathetic pat.

When play finally resumed, we just stalled, playing slow, time-wasting football until the end of the game. San Cristobal never came back.

Being back in the locker room didn't feel the way I'd expected it to. Everybody was definitely up, cheerful and bubbly. Guys kept slapping me on the backside and high-fiving me, but I couldn't seem to get in the mood. In the shower, I kept thinking about Suarez in the hospital and the other guy with his leg wrecked—maybe as bad as Gibbs's.

They'd gone out ready to get hurt, sure. But they didn't

know about lifting, or how the Effect could turn a guy into a battering ram. So I didn't exactly feel like a conquering hero about my heroic conquests.

The weedy young guy from the radio station was in the locker room while I was getting dressed. He introduced himself, stuck a microphone in my face, and asked how it felt to score five touchdowns in one evening.

I could've said something smart-ass, like "Quintuple the feeling of scoring one touchdown"; instead, I just muttered that it felt okay.

"Nobody could believe your speed, Rick," they guy said with a big grin full of brown teeth. "And you're clearly not intimidated by your opponents, no matter how big they are. What's your secret?"

Out of sheer nerves, I nearly lifted then and there.

"I dunno," I said. "I guess if you're moving fast enough, you'll get through. Uh, excuse me, I've got to meet some friends."

He didn't want to go away, but Gibbs loomed up and shooed him.

"You did very well tonight, Stevenson."

"Thanks, Mr. Gibbs."

"Feeling a little down?"

"Well, yeah. About the guys who got hurt."

"It happens. Just one of the risks we all run. With a different set of breaks, it could've been you on that stretcher." He gripped my shoulder for a moment and looked into my eyes. It crossed my mind that *he'd* been on a stretcher once, and now he was looking for someone else to do the things he couldn't do on the field anymore. "I'm not going to try to tell you to forget about it. Just try to keep it in perspective."

"Yes, sir."

I finished getting dressed and waded out through crowds of fans. Flashbulbs were going off in my face, and a couple of tenth-graders even asked for my autograph. I felt silly, especially when Pat and Melinda started waving on the edge of the crowd.

"Hey, there he is!" Melinda yelled. "Wow!" I struggled through the mob to reach them, and she hugged me. "Were you ever great! I couldn't believe it. I think I've wrecked my voice. How did you learn to run like that?"

"Chasing Marcus. Hi," I said to Pat. She grinned and gave me a thump on the chest with the handle of her cane.

"What d'you guys want to do now?" Melinda asked. "Go get a pizza, or what?"

"Let's just go home and take it easy," I said. "I've had enough for one night. Besides, Pat and I are going on a hike tomorrow, so we better make it an early night."

"Your wish is my command."

This was a side of my mother's personality I wasn't too happy to learn about. At least Pat was keeping her cool. We went off to the parking lot with Melinda on my left arm and Pat on my right; Melinda drove us home in her old beige Volvo station wagon.

We had a quiet, comfortable hour or so, listening to Mozart and Vivaldi while we drank tea and ate huge slabs of spice cake. The conversation was easy and animated, even though I didn't say much. Pat and Melinda chattered away about the game and the music and the cake; every once in a while, Pat caught my eye and winked. Finally, around 10:30, I yawned and said it was time to take Pat home.

"Well, drive carefully," said Melinda. "I won't wait up for you—I'm pooped." She walked us to the door, chatting while I helped Pat on with her duffel coat. "It was fun, wasn't it? I never thought I'd end up a football groupie. Where are you guys going hiking tomorrow?"

"San Miguel Creek, I guess," I said.

"D'you mind if I keep Marcus? He's supposed to go in for his shots, and I can take him up to Hillside Park after."

"Okay," I shrugged, delighted. For what we had planned tomorrow, Marcus would have had to be left in the car anyway.

"And let's have Pat for supper when you guys get back."

"Sure," I agreed.

"Only if I can cook it," Pat said.

"It's a deal," I said quickly. I'd seen Melinda's eyes light up; give her a chance and she'd spend another hour working out a menu, discussing the pros and cons of homemade pasta, and reminiscing about Pat's earlier culinary triumphs.

"I'll talk to you in the morning," Pat promised. "Thanks, Melinda."

Five minutes later, we were up at Hillside Park, pulling on mittens and balaclavas.

"Those jeans going to be warm enough?" I worried.

"I put on tights underneath." Pat giggled. "This is a riot."

"What?"

"Sitting parked in a car with my boyfriend, and we're both putting on *more* clothes."

"You can go bare naked if you want to," I said, "but the goose pimples will make a lot of air resistance."

"I'll show you one thing I'm not wearing." She unstrapped her brace and heaved it into the back seat. Then she let herself out of the car, balancing a little unsurely with the help of the Effect. I got out and came around to her; she took my hand.

"All day I've been waiting for this," Pat whispered.

"Me, too." I was shivering a little, and not just from the chill in the air. I looked around. We were parked near the lookout where we'd first had lunch, weeks ago. No other cars were around, but we were close to street lights and the road.

"Come on," I said. Holding hands, we walked into the darkness under a stand of aspens. Pat's leg swung a little awkwardly, but she was *walking*, with no brace, no cane.

"Are we really going up there?"

"Don't be scared. Just wait until you see the view."

And up we went, still holding hands.

For the first hundred feet, Pat clung tightly to my hand. Then, as she gained confidence, her fingers loosened. Santa Teresa spread out below us, a glittering network of lights. I could see Las Estacas Street, and my own darkened house; a mile away was Pat's place, all lit up. The hum of traffic was clear, and we could hear music playing somewhere close below.

We didn't talk much, except to point things out to each other: a jogger shuffling through the pool of light around a street lamp, a police car speeding down a road with its red and blue lights flashing wildly. Slowly, steadily, we rose through ragged low clouds into a blue-gray world of moonlight and stars. The wind tugged at us and we went with it, matching its speed and direction so that we seemed to hang motionless. For a long time we let the wind carry us, while we watched clouds shift and change in the half-moon's light. Far below, a light or two gleamed through breaks in the cloud.

Pat turned to me and put her arms around my neck. Her face was a pale oval, her eyes bright in the moonlight. We held each other close, each enjoying the other's warmth.

"We're free, Rick. We're the only free people in the whole world."

I hugged her and kissed her as we glided damply through a cloud, but I didn't say anything. I was happier than I'd ever been in my life, but I felt somehow that it wasn't going to last, that I was becoming less free all the time.

10

I DIDN'T SLEEP well that night. The last twenty-four hours had been too eventful, and my mind kept racing from the fight with Jason to the collision with Al Suarez to the first glimpse of Pat lifting off the bed. Or maybe I was asleep after all, and just dreaming; at one point, I know, I did have a flying dream and woke to find myself solidly in bed. That was a relief. The Effect might need a theta state to get you started, but you couldn't lift in your sleep.

The Saturday dawn was gray and drizzly. I was up even before Melinda, and made myself some oatmeal for breakfast. As usual I read the paper while I ate, but for once I started with the sports section. It was mostly about the game, and featured a big photo of me lifting over the San Cristobal tackler, with a caption that read something like: "Terry High back Rick Stevenson rockets over San Cristobal defender en route to 5 touchdowns. Terry High Saints look good for the Central Conference title if they can take San Carlos next week and beat Calaveras the week after."

The story itself made me feel uncomfortable. I was used to reading about myself on electronic bulletin boards, where I generally appeared under the *nom de guerre* of Doctor Dork, but here was a story with my real name in it, and all kinds of corny writing about how fast I was and how San Cristobal looked as if they were standing still. Not on the field, they hadn't! Apparently I'd also set a record for yards gained in a single game.

It even spent a paragraph on Al Suarez and the other guy, Scott Smith. Suarez was in Santa Teresa General with unde- termined internal injuries, and Smith had torn cartilage in his right knee. The story didn't spend a whole lot of sympathy on them.

After finishing the paper, I just sat there in the kitchen and looked at the rain oozing out of a dull sky. Eventually Melinda came downstairs and snatched the paper off the table. Before she'd finished reciting the purpler passages, the phone rang.

It wasn't Pat; it was some guy I didn't know, a Terry High alumnus (class of '54) who said he was really proud of me and keep up the great work. I thanked him and hung up, and the phone rang again. It was the manager of a sporting goods store downtown who said he just wanted to congratulate me on a fine job, and anytime I needed sporting goods he'd give me a fifteen percent discount. I thanked him, and hung up, and the phone rang again.

"H'lo?" I barked.

"*Wow,*" Pat said. "What's the matter with *you* today?"

"Oh, hi. I'm sorry. I just got two calls back to back from people I never heard of, and it's not even eight o'clock yet. How are you?"

"Rarin' to go if you are."

"I'll be over before you know it."

"Goody."

Leaving the phone off the hook, I started throwing stuff into my backpack: some gorp, some apples, a hunk of sausage and some rolls, stuff like that. Melinda was so deep in her print trance that she hardly noticed until I was ready to leave.

"You're going hiking."

"Is that an observation or a command?"

"Where to, may I ask, in case we have to send out the bloodhounds?"

"It's no challenge for them if they know where I've gone,

so I'll lie and say San Miguel Creek."

"Okay. You're sure Pat's up to it, with this rain and all?"

"She did fine last time, and she's in better shape this week. Especially after all that jumping around and screaming you two were doing last night."

"After all that jumping around and screaming, I can hardly hold my head up this morning. You say we have to go through the whole thing again next week?"

"Next week *I* sit in the stands and *you* get to play."

"Nobody loves a smart-ass football hero. Go get your girl-friend and get lost."

I had hardly pulled away from the curb in front of Pat's house when she began undoing her brace.

"Oh, that feels good. I can't wait to race you up the creek."

It was hard to keep my eyes on the road, her face was so radiant and happy. Shifting was hard, too, since we kept hold-ing hands. The drizzle kept up; Brunhilde's windshield defog-ger sighed helplessly. We buzzed through empty, shiny streets, out past the city airport.

"Look!" Pat exclaimed. "Parachutes."

I braked and squinted through the misty windshield. A few hundred feet up, a light plane was droning past as it disgorged a string of skydivers. Each one dropped, a black speck, for long seconds before suddenly blooming into a flower, bright orange or striped red and white, vivid against the gray sky. They seemed to be aiming for a target zone beyond the main runway, where a few cars and trucks were surrounded by peo-ple in rain slickers or jump suits.

"God, that must take real guts," Pat said.

I started the car up again. "Never get me up in one of those things," I agreed.

We drove on, listening to boring old Pachelbel's canon on the tape deck and chatting about this and that. Before long we reached the parking lot on San Miguel Creek. It was deserted. The clouds were low enough to cut off the tops of the hills; a damp, chilly wind blew down the canyon in our faces. Bare aspens shivered against the clouds.

Pat couldn't have cared less. After a quick look around, she took off up the trail in long, gliding strides. She was learning how to use the Effect to control the movement of her bad leg without interfering with her good one, and she moved gracefully. I followed her, and took a good half mile to catch up.

"Don't overdo it," I warned. "You could come around a curve in the trail and bump into somebody who isn't ready for a girl who walks like Carl Lewis jumps."

"Okay."

So we drifted along, holding hands and enjoying the fine drizzle in our faces. The creek bellowed away below us, and before we knew it we'd reached the spot where Pat had slipped. She paused when we looked down the slope.

"Some day they'll put up a historical plaque here," she said, grinning, as she turned to me. "That seems so long ago, Rick, and it was just a week. It feels like it happened to somebody else."

"It did," I said, and kissed her.

We went on, up into the mist where visibility was just a few feet. "Let's see how high we can jump," I suggested. "One, two—three!"

And up we went.

The ground vanished within seconds; we were climbing through a wet gray nothing, listening to the rush of the creek and the hum of the wind in the pines below us. My ears popped.

"How high are we?" Pat asked.

I checked the altimeter. "Four hundred feet above ground level. Four twenty-five. Four fifty."

We were almost two thousand feet above ground level, and maybe five thousand above sea level, when we broke through the top of the cloud deck into dazzling sunshine. To the south and west and north, the white plain stretched to the horizon, marked only here and there by a tuft or wisp standing out against the perfect deep blue of the sky. To the east, the Sierra Nevada jutted up, many miles away, yet looking close enough to touch. Their peaks and ridges were blazingly white, almost too bright to look at.

Pat reached into her jacket and pulled out two pairs of ski goggles. "I thought it might be a little bright up here."

"Boy, are you ever smart." I pulled my goggles on grate-fully; the albedo of the clouds and mountains was something fierce.

For a few minutes we just hung there, holding hands and looking at the slow movements of the clouds and listening to the silence.

It was quiet up there. Not dead quiet; we could still faintly hear the creek far below us, and a murmur of wind. But those soft sounds only made the stillness that much deeper.

"I could stay here forever," Pat said. With nothing to echo from, her voice sounded small and flat.

"Forever isn't long enough." I put my arms around her and squeezed. "Let's just drift for a while."

So we let the wind carry us gently eastward, less than fifty feet above the cloud tops. We floated horizontally, on our sides, so we could see each other. We talked and laughed; when we got hungry, we floated on our backs and used our stomachs as tables for a picnic of apples and sausage sandwiches.

"This is fine," said Pat. "Maybe we should keep it to our-selves." She was nestled against me now, her head resting on my arm. The sun was warm on us, though the air was cold. "We're the only two people in the world."

"Not exactly. Look off to the west." I pointed to the distant gleam of sunlight on a plane's fuselage: probably a jetliner headed for Sacramento.

"That doesn't count. But some day the sky will be full of people; and we'll miss the good old days when we had it all."

"You know," I said, "maybe we *should* keep it to our-selves."

"What for?"

"Oh . . . I think about what could happen when everybody can lift."

"Like what?"

"Like muggers and rapists coming at you out of the sky, anywhere you happen to be. Armies invading other countries. Refugees going whatever they think they'll be safe. Real chaos."

"Anybody comes after me, I'll slam him the way you slammed those guys in the game."

"Yeah, and that's something else. You can really hurt people with the Effect. I didn't mean to hurt those guys, at least not the way I did. But somebody who knows karate, for instance—and also knows how to lift—boy, he could be dangerous. It's a lot of power to give somebody."

"Well, everybody else'll have it, too. It'll all even out."

"Will it, Pat? We don't know that. I've been thinking about other things, too. Like what happens to the economy when everybody can lift. Who'll buy cars? Or ride on buses? If the auto industry goes under, what happens to everything else? Do the airlines survive? Do the highways start falling apart? What happens to the environment when millions of people start looking for their own little patch of wilderness and they turn it all into a garbage dump? Maybe you're ready for a lifting rapist, but is a grizzly bear ready for a lifting hunter?"

"I thought you were only scared about people on the *ground* with guns."

"I am. When the nuts get airborne, I'll be even more scared. This'll be like giving a loaded gun to an idiot child."

"That's crap. Who says people are idiots?"

"Some are, Pat. Too many."

"And you're one of them. Let me tell you a story. This teenage cave man is sitting around banging flints together one day, just for laughs, and strikes a spark and the spark starts a fire. It's warm, it's bright, it's a really nice fire. But the cave man sits there warming his hands and maybe cooking a nice lizard, and he thinks: In the wrong hands, like those Neanderthals in the next cave, fire would be a real pain. The Neanderthals will throw burning sticks on us good guys. And they'll start forest fires. Maybe they'll learn how to burn tobacco and give everybody lung cancer. So he pees on his fire, and it goes out."

"That's a pretty shaky argument," I answered, because I didn't think it was.

"The hell it is. You've stumbled on something as important as fire, or electromagnetism, and you're just going to for*get* about it?"

"If it's like fire or electromagnetism, somebody else will discover it soon enough. And then I won't be responsible for the problems."

Pat burst into that staccato laugh of hers. "You're two thousand feet up in the air, talking about the problems of lifting! Practice what you preach, you turkey."

"Quiet."

"Huh?"

"Sh."

I'd heard something: a distant rumble, coming closer. Now we both heard it and looked around for its source.

A jet fighter suddenly shot out of the clouds just a couple of miles away. It was an F-14, sleek and powerful and unbelievably fast. I watched it the way a sparrow must watch a stooping hawk—unblinkingly, bewildered by the attacker's might and unable to imagine all that energy devoted to catching something so much smaller and weaker. Watching a jet from the ground is watching a machine; watching it from the air is watching something alive.

"Drop!" I shouted, and turned off the Effect. The Effect around Pat vanished an instant later, and we began to fall. From the corner of my eye I could see the jet circle toward us. Then we were plunging headfirst through the clouds, holding tight to each other. The jet crashed past overhead, so loud we yelled inaudibly in fright. I turned on the Effect again to drive us down faster than mere gravity could. Then we were below the clouds, diving toward forested hills.

"Get ready to slow," I said. Pat nodded; as long as we held on to each other, if only one of us braked, the other would tear free and keep falling. "One; two; *three*."

It was bumpy, but we got down to a reasonable speed. First the deceleration drove blood into our heads, nearly blacking us out; then, as we pivoted so we were falling feet first, the blood drained from our heads just the way it does when you've been squatting for a long time and you stand up suddenly. When I got over feeling dizzy, I looked around for landmarks and finally, off in the distance, saw what must be the highway. We'd come quite a few miles east of San Miguel Creek.

Now we soared back up through the rain into the overcast, heading west. Above us the jet's engines faded like thunder and then grew loud again.

Pat and I were still holding each other tight, even though it slowed us down. "He's hunting us," I said into her ear.

She stared at me, her eyes barely visible through the ski goggles.

"The air force knows something's going on out here. That's what Gassaway's been going on about. I got them to chase me when I buzzed the control tower. But I never thought they'd pick us up so far from the base, or send one of those damn huge things after us."

Inside the strange, effervescent sheath of the Effect, I was shivering. We were vulnerable, fragile as butterflies; we could not only be caught and unmasked, we could be killed. They would have a great time wondering how two teenage misfits had gotten sucked into the slipstream of an F-14, a thousand feet or so above the earth, and torn to bits.

We began to rollercoast, dipping below the overcast and rising again, looking for San Miguel Creek without spending too much time being visible. Once we were back with Brunhilde, we'd be safe—just another ordinary couple coming home from an ordinary hike. But it felt like a long time before we finally found the creek. Brunhilde was alone in the parking lot, but we took no chances. The overcast was still low over the hills here, and we glided slowly through the mist until the slope rose up under our feet. We sank to earth on the trail and took off downhill.

"Can they still see us on radar?" Pat asked.

"I doubt it. Once we got close to the ground, we blurred into the background." At least I hoped we had; my respect for air force electronics had risen sharply in the last few minutes.

The puddled parking lot looked just as it had when we'd left it. Half-expecting CIA agents to pop out from behind the trees, I unlocked Brunhilde and we got in. Pat looked at me and burst out laughing. I laughed, too. It's not every day you get chased by a jet fighter, and escape.

We spent the rest of the day exploring other trails in the hills, but minding our manners and giving the air force no reason to spend taxpayers' dollars hunting us. On empty trails in the endless drizzle, we covered a lot of ground in long strides, occasionally lifting to inspect a hawk's nest or to cross a creek. When the drizzle turned to steady rain we went back to the car and listened to tapes, and then we went home.

About the time we got into town, Pat asked: "Are you serious about not telling anybody about lifting?"

"I don't know. I'm just worried about the harm it could do."

"Don't. Worry about getting fat on the lasagna I'm going to make for dinner."

The rest of the afternoon was agreeably domestic: Pat and Melinda made acres of lasagna in the kitchen, while I vegetated with the evening paper.

It wasn't as full of stuff about the game, since it was a Sacramento paper, but it had a fairly long story about "Terry High's startling rookie back." I read it and went on to the real news, but not with much attention. Instead I sat there thinking about Al Suarez and Scott Smith, and wondering whether the pilot of the F-14 had actually seen us. If he had, had he told his bosses what he'd seen? If he had, was he now in a rubber room?

Dinner was good, and we had a pleasant time until Pat said she was tired and could I take her home. So we took our usual route home, via Hillside Park, and Pat whipped off her brace again.

"At this rate, you're going to need something like a ski binding."

"This stupid thing's days are numbered. Come on, let's get out there and chase bats."

"And you sure it's smart, Pat? I don't want to dodge any more jets, and if we turn up on radar a couple more times, Bobby Gassaway will go into convulsions."

"How will they be able to tell? C'mon, don't be a party pooper."

"Okay, okay." So we left Brunhilde and walked up into a grove of trees. The rain had stopped at last, but it was wet underfoot and deserted as usual. Pat didn't bother with a balaclava or anything; she just said "Shazam!" and took off straight up, leaving me to follow.

I was nervous as hell, but that faded once I was off the ground. It was so good to lift, to soar up and see the city lights rotate below, and then to feel Pat's hand in mine. We went up only about five hundred feet, and didn't move away from the park; it was fun just to do somersaults and slow rolls, and I didn't want to be too far from the car if the air force crashed the party again.

After we'd been up a few minutes, I saw a car drive past the park, slow, and then do a U-turn into the parking lot. Probably some horny couple, I supposed, until it rolled under a street light and I recognized Jason Murphy's white Trans Am. It parked right next to Brunhilde. Jason's tape deck was blasting away, and it got even louder when the car doors opened and a couple of people got out.

"Look," I said quietly. "Jason."

"That fink. Did he recognize your car?"

"He must have." It was easy enough; how many old red VWs have a bumper sticker that asks: "Have You Hugged Your Nerd Today?"

One of the two guys went to the trunk of the Trans Am and then came back to the other guy. I saw them swing their arms against Brunhilde's windshield, and heard glass shatter.

"Those—"

I nearly shouted out loud in rage and frustration. Jason and his Tricycle Rat friend smashed every window in Brunhilde while we watched, helpless. They probably would have gone on to slash her tires or even set her afire, but must have decided that the noise they were making would attract Pat and me out of the underbrush in time to identify them. So thirty seconds after the attack started, they were back in Jason's car and peeling out of the parking lot, headed uphill onto Skyline Road.

"I'll be right back," I snarled, and shot downward, following the Trans Am.

"I'm coming, too. Don't do anything stupid," Pat said.

Head down, with my fists in my pockets, I caught up quickly with Jason, who was taking the sharp curves on Skyline fairly carefully. I could hear his tape deck blaring with the same kind of idiot noise that Pat's roommates got off on. The car was the only one on the road, which was encouraging.

Swinging into a feet-down position, I matched speed with the Trans Am and landed on its roof with a satisfyingly loud thump. The Vibram soles on my hiking boots put a respectable dent in the metal.

But the best part was the simultaneous shrieks from Jason
and his buddy and the car's brakes. I slowed even faster than
the car did, fell behind, then accelerated feet first into the
Trans Am's rear window. It was tougher than I'd expected,
and didn't shatter, but a couple of large cracks flashed out
from under my boots. I went back onto the roof and did some
flamenco dancing, drumming my heels until the whole roof
was stamped in and mottled with boot prints.

Jason had accelerated again after I hit the rear window, but
now he hit the brakes and went into a long, screaming skid on
the wet road. To one side was a steep hillside; to the other was
an even steeper drop into a canyon; straight ahead was a hair-
pin turn. I lifted up some twenty or thirty feet and saw the
Trans Am's rear end smack into a telephone pole. The whole
car whipped around and slammed nose-first, hard, into a shallow ditch on the uphill side. Its headlights were still on, and
enough light reflected from the hillside to show Jason and his
half-wit buddy crawling out of the car.

"Omigod! Omigod! Omigod!" Jason kept saying. "Omigod, my dad'll kill me! Omigod! What was it? What was it?"
His buddy just groaned.

I hadn't heard a male duet so beautiful since Tucker and
Bjoerling's "Au Fond du Temple Sacre" from *The Pearl
Fishers*. When Jason's wails rose to high C as he ran his paws
over the dented roof of the Trans Am, I nearly burst into
applause.

Then his buddy leaned over the hood and said: "Hey,
Jason, I don't feel so good."

Jason stopped yelping and went over to him.

"Jeezus, Brad, you're bleeding!"

"I think I hit the windshield. Jeez, it's running down inside
my shirt and all. Jason—I don't feel so good." And he threw
up all over the hood.

Pat was beside me, hovering in the dark. I turned to her,
and suddenly I didn't feel so great myself. "Let's go," I murmured. "I'll phone for an ambulance."

Squinting through poor Brunhilde's smashed windshield, I
pulled into the parking lot of a 7-Eleven and found a public
phone; I dialed 911 and reported an auto accident on Skyline,

then hung up without identifying myself. I got back in the car and drove Pat home; we didn't talk much until we'd stopped outside her house.

I turned off the ignition and sighed. "I think I scared myself silly up there."

Her hand was warm on my face. "Just be glad it wasn't worse."

"It only shows that idiots shouldn't be allowed to lift."

"You lost your temper, Rick, and I don't blame you. After what those creeps did, they deserved what they got."

"They didn't deserve to get killed, and they damn near were," I answered thickly.

"Don't eat your heart out, Rick. *Please*. You got mad and you hit out at them, and we all learned something. What do you want to do, turn yourself in to the cops for malicious mischief? Or flying without a license?"

I laughed. It sounded like somebody being garrotted.

"Go home and get some sleep," Pat said. "We've had a rough day." She gave me a kiss and swung out of the car. When she was halfway down the walk to her front door, I did a double take.

"Hey!" I hissed.

"What?"

"You forgot your brace."

"Oops!" She popped back in and wrestled herself into it. "See you tomorrow?"

"In the afternoon. Maybe around two or three. I've got to go to the hospital before that."

"What for?"

"Pay a visit to Al Suarez."

11

"RICK—WHAT'S *happened* to your *car*?"

Melinda was so upset she'd actually barged into my room. I opened my eyes and blinked at her while Marcus stood up and stretched beside the bed.

"I got vandalized last night," I mumbled.

"What? How?"

"I took Pat home and then I went up to Hillside Park and went for a walk. When I got back, somebody'd broken all the windows."

"My *God*. What on earth possessed you to go for a walk in the park in the middle of the night when it's freezing out?"

I rolled out of bed and pulled on my jeans. "Well, it's been kind of a wild week, Melinda. I just needed a little time to think about things."

"What's wrong with thinking right here at home? You think here, nobody's going to break your windows while you're doing it. Hillside Park is no place to be after dark."

"So I've learned."

"Well, you'll have to call the insurance people and get it all cleared up. That car's your responsiblity, you know." She shook her head. "What a bummer. Well, come on down and have some breakfast."

Pulling on my favorite red-and-black checked flannel shirt, I trudged downstairs. The kitchen smelled good: Melinda was baking blueberry muffins. She grilled me some more about the car, but I'd worked out my story and stuck to it.

"What a bummer," she repeated. "I'd sure like to get my hands on the jerk who did it. When I looked out this morning and saw it like that, I couldn't believe my eyes. God, I hate that kind of pointless violence."

"That makes two of us."

"You're taking it a lot more calmly than I thought you would."

"You should've seen me last night."

I ate my breakfast and looked out at the gray sky. A jet boomed past overhead. The weather looked raw and chilly.

"What are you up to today? Pat coming over?"

"Later. I have to go out and see Al Suarez this morning. The guy I put in the hospital."

"Oh. That's really nice of you, Rick. But you didn't really put him in the hospital, you know. That was just the breaks."

"Yeah, well."

After breakfast I did a lot of chores and then took Marcus for a long walk. I'd neglected him lately, but he didn't hold a grudge. We went up Las Estacas Street to where it ended on the edge of a little canyon, and then went up the canyon into the scrub pine that dotted the dull brown hillside. Marcus bounded back and forth, running ahead and then racing back to make sure I was okay, so he ended up covering four times the distance I did.

It was a steep climb, and the slope was muddy after the rain; before long my legs were aching, and I was puffing. Walking was hard work. No one was around—I couldn't even see any houses—but I resisted the urge to lift. It wasn't easy.

When we got back, I showered and dressed in more presentable clothes: blue slacks, a blue-and-white striped shirt, my best Harris tweed sport coat. Then I went out to poor Brunhilde and drove to the hospital. The windshield had two quarter-sized holes in it, surrounded by spiderwebbed cracks, which made it both hard to see and pretty cold.

Never having been in the hospital before, I took awhile to find Al Suarez. The place depressed me. It was full of people on crutches, people in wheelchairs, people lying in bed staring at TV or the ceiling. Finally I found him, in a ward with six other people, all old men. He was sitting up, his bed cranked up under his back, and he was reading a murder mystery. He looked bigger in bed than he had on the field, with huge broad shoulders and knuckly hands. He was wearing a neck brace, and his chest, under a hospital bathrobe, was taped.

"Hi,". I said, stopping at the foot of the bed. "I'm Rick Stevenson. Number 77, remember? How are you?"

He looked surprised to see me, but he wasn't angry.

"Uh, okay, I guess. Well, not exactly, but I'm feeling better than I did yesterday." He waved me to a chair beside his bed, and shook my hand as I sat down. "Thanks for coming. Hey, you got a lot of coverage in the paper."

"Yeah. This town has a thing about football. I'm glad you're feeling better."

"Well, you really hit me a good one." He pointed to his chest. "You know I got three cracked ribs?"

"Oh no! I'm really sorry."

"Lot of internal bleeding, too, but they got that stopped. If it wasn't for that, they'd've sent me home already. But they're scared I'm gonna start bleedin' again."

"Boy, I sure hope not."

"You and me both, man. Man, that was scary. I never peed red before. Listen, let me ask you something."

"Sure."

"On that play, you know? You had plenty of room to get around me, 'specially you being so fast and all. But you just came straight for me, like you wanted to take me out. Is that what you really wanted to do? Just put me outa the game?"

"Oh no, no—I really didn't. I just—I knew you guys were gonna really go after me unless I showed I could go after *you*, you know?"

He could understand that. "Took a lot of guts, man. So you were just tryin' to psych us out, huh?"

"Sort of."

"Well, I guess it worked. Some of the guys from the team were in yesterday and geez, they were really down about it.

They got kind of scared of you, you know?"

He didn't realize how bizarre that sounded: great big jocks scared of Supernerd. "Well, uh, that was the idea," I said. I didn't say *whose* idea.

"Yeah, well, we ever play you again, we'll put your ass in a sling right away."

"I ever play *you* again, I'll be moving so fast you won't even *see* my ass."

He started laughing, but it turned to a choked growl and a grimace. "Geez, these ribs really hurt."

"But only when you laugh?"

"Yeah. Too bad I got a great sense of humor."

"What's the neck brace for?"

"Whiplash."

*"Whip*lash?"

"Can you believe it? I must've been asleep when you came at me."

We talked for a few more minutes, but I wasn't really paying attention. A little more oomph in the Effect on Friday night, and this nice big guy might now be lying in a funeral parlor in San Cristobal, with a broken neck or a burst aorta or who knew what, and on Monday morning his family would bury him. I would have a couple of broken ribs instead of just a few bruises, and I wouldn't be cracking jokes. I'd probably be talking to cops who figured I was zonked on steroids or something.

Finally I left. Al shook my hand and thanked me for coming by; I said I'd try to make it back in a day or two. Then I crept out of the hospital, feeling terrible.

The insurance guy came around just as Melinda and I were finishing lunch; he wasn't annoyed at having to work on a Sunday, and even accepted a corned beef on rye. Still eating, he walked back out to the sidewalk with me and examined Brunhilde.

"Seen worse," he commented. "Usually they pick expensive cars, Mercedes, Porsches, something they can't even dream of having. Guess they figured your car'd do for practice." He filled out a form and gave me the carbon. "Better file an accident report with the police. Otherwise you'll have a tough time getting the repairs done."

So I took poor Brunhilde downtown to the cop shop and filled out a long form. The cop who came outside with me to confirm the damage seemed depressed.

"What a shame, after that great game you played Friday. Vandalism, it's the curse of the twentieth century. Nothing's sacred any more, not even a person's personal automobile. No one respects property rights. Another five years and we'll be living under communism, if the dope dealers don't take over first."

By now I was feeling so down I was grateful even for sympathy from a lunatic policeman. I cheered up a little more when I picked up Pat, who was feeling fine. When she learned I hadn't done any homework in days, she declared a state of siege.

"We're going to get you caught up by dinnertime, or you get no dinner and Melinda and I will pig out."

"Hey, what's with the threats?"

"I'm not going to risk my reputation by going around with some rangitang jock who flunks everything."

"If I hear one more reference to athletics today," I growled, "I'll show you *real* rangitang."

"Now who's into threats?" And she leaned over and kissed me.

"If you insist on smelling that good, you're going to have to keep your distance."

My slowly rising spirits lost what little Effect they had when I got home and Melinda, working in the study, said Bobby Gassaway had called and would I phone him back. I did.

"Hey," said Gassaway, "they saw some more UFOs Friday and yesterday. Know anything about 'em?"

"Not until you tell me."

"You sure? You're not doing kites or model airplanes or hot-air balloons or anything?"

"Gimme a break, Gassaway."

"The finger of suspicion points to you, Stevenson," he said in mock-portentous tones. "I think you're running some heavy hoax, and the air force is getting annoyed about it."

"Gassaway, there is no hoax."

"How do you know?"

"Shut up, Gassaway."

"I've been watching you, Stevenson. You're a big b.s. artist. First it's computer crime, now it's UFO hoaxes. You've got a sick sense of humor."

I looked at Pat and rolled my eyes. "If I did, I'd think you were funnier than you are. Talk to you tomorrow, Gassaway, if the little green men don't get you first."

As we went upstairs, Pat asked: "What was that all about?"

"Bobby smells a rat. He's really convinced I'm hoaxing the air force and his daddy."

"So what?"

"It makes me nervous. I think about that jet coming up out of the clouds, and I get the shivers. Maybe they saw us. For all I know, they took photos of us."

"What if they did? We weren't doing anything wrong."

I wasn't in the mood for wisecracks. We went into my room and I slouched into my desk chair while Pat lifted herself smoothly into the old overstuffed armchair in the corner.

"I'm just starting to feel a little paranoid about all this, Pat. We aren't exactly being discreet about lifting. We turn up on radar like the swallows coming back to Capistrano. I bashed into Al Suarez so hard I could've killed him. I nearly killed Jason and whatsisface, and I left some dents in his car that people might get really curious about."

"Boloney. Occam's razor. Even if Jason told what happened, who'd believe him? They'd figure it was more likely that he was ripped out of his skull, cracked up the car, and then jumped up and down on the roof for a giggle."

"Maybe so," I agreed, "but the point remains that we're fooling around with something really powerful, and it's awfully easy to start abusing it. It's kind of like having a pistol around the house—it can turn any little dispute into murder. I've got into a whole string of little fights with Jason, and each time I end up using the Effect in a more violent way."

"He's a slow learner."

"Being an idiot isn't a capital offense, and I'm not the State of California; I've got no right to kill people I don't like."

"You're a slow learner, too. But you *are* learning, Rick. We both are. My gosh, we're brand new at all this; we're lucky we haven't killed ourselves, let alone Jason. Do you think you're really such a psycho case that you'll end up murdering everybody who looks cross-eyed at you?"

"No. But other people sometimes really are psycho cases."

"We're back to that, huh?"

"I guess so. Well, imagine it was Jason who could lift. Suppose he decided to jump on Brunhilde's roof; think he'd care if I drove us off a cliff? He'd laugh. And there's a million Jasons out there. Think about the loonies who go up in office towers, or into hamburger joints, with a couple of rifles and a thousand rounds, and start killing everybody in sight. Imagine a guy like that, lifting down Market Street in San Francisco with an M-16." I lifted my hands helplessly. "Pat, this is too much power for an ordinary jerk like me."

"Or me?"

"Or you, or anybody. Look, you and I proved it's easy to teach lifting, easier than catching a cold. If we go public with this, we have to start teaching other people, and *they* teach other people. It spreads geometrically, and eventually some people learn it who are going to go crazy with it. If we go to the government and say, here's a secret, we still have to teach people and the same thing finally happens. My gosh, I'll bet you wouldn't even have to be taught by a lifter—if you know how it's done the first time, you can do it by yourself. Like building an atomic bomb."

Pat sat quietly in the armchair, her hands folded in her lap. I belatedly noticed that she was wearing black pants and a dark blue sweater, and I was suddenly willing to bet that her backpack held goggles and a balaclava as well as her school books. She was all ready to go lifting tonight.

"You think about the crazies," she said at last. "I think about the people like me. Rick, I'm sixteen years old, and I never took a step without help until you taught me how to lift. All my life I've been a prisoner of a stupid hip. Sometimes at night, I used to lie in bed and try to jump out of my own body—just leave it behind, so I could be free, so I wouldn't have to limp and I wouldn't have to hurt all the time. And now I *am* free. At least some of the time, I'm as free as a bird. I think you want me to be back in my cage, and wear this damn thing"—she slapped her brace—"the rest of my life. And you want everybody like me to stay in their cages, too.

Do you know how many people can't walk at all? Amputees, people with strokes, paraplegics and quadraplegics and people with cerebral palsy and old ladies with brittle bones who fall down and break their hips. Teach them how to lift, and they can do *anything*. They can live the way they're supposed to live. It'd be the greatest miracle cure in history. Even if I knew some nut was going to shoot me after I'd been lifting for just a day, a day of freedom would be better than a lifetime in a cage, or a brace, or a wheelchair. An *hour* of freedom."

I didn't quite know what to say to that, so I just shook my head slowly, to gain time.

"It's not that simple, Pat. Heck, you don't even know if some of the people you mentioned could lift anyway. Suppose if you've got a stroke or palsy or something like that, you can't lift; how would you feel when you saw other people lifting out of wheelchairs?"

"I'd feel terrible. But at least there wouldn't be so many people like me. The misery level would drop a lot."

"Maybe on the personal side it would. On the social side it would start going up pretty soon after." She started to speak, but I went on: "Pat—I think I understand, I really think I do. But you've got to understand how I feel, too. Which is *scared.*" I could hardly speak the last word. I was shivering, and noticed—as if from a distance—that my palms were pressed together between my knees. "I've got to work this all out somehow, so I know I'm doing the right thing, so I don't spend the rest of my life regretting all this ever happened."

"So what do you want to do?" Pat's voice was calm.

"I'm going to give up lifting for a while."

"Completely?"

"Completely."

"For how long?"

"For however long it takes me to figure things out. If I go on lifting, it'd be like smoking while I tried to decide if I should quit."

She laughed, briefly. "Boy, Gibbs would skin you alive if you tried out that kind of argument by analogy with him."

"Maybe. But it really is like a drug."

"Sure, like oxygen or food. Really addictive. And what am I supposed to do while you're working this out?"

"I can't tell you what to do. But one reason I'm going to quit is so I don't get caught and have to reveal everything. I just hope you don't attract more attention from the air force or whoever."

She looked out the window at the willow tree's branches brushing against the glass. "I think I can do that much."

"Okay. Good. Now how about some homework?"

"Fair enough."

We got into it, and I felt a little better. But even with Pat sitting right next to me, I had a funny feeling that she was a long, long way away.

12

THE AFTERNOON AND evening passed quietly, with homework and preparing dinner and eating it and going out to rent a movie and coming back and watching it and finally taking Pat home. She kissed me good-night in the car.

"See you tomorrow morning," I said.

"Great."

"I love you, you know."

I think she must've known I wasn't saying it just to be lovey-dovey, but to make her do things my way. I'd already decided that all was fair in love, war, and levitation. But she didn't bite my head off or anything; she just kissed me again and went inside.

I drove home and sat in my room reading science fiction until one in the morning, bored out of my skull. All that empty sky up there, and me not in it, and Pat probably out soloing . . .

But the air base was quiet. Maybe she'd decided it was smarter not to taunt them so soon after they'd nearly caught us. I fell asleep and dreamed about lifting.

Monday morning was cold, with sunshine burning through

a high overcast. Between the shattered windshield and Brunhilde's feeble defroster, I could hardly see where I was going.
Pat limped out from the house and got in.

"Hi again," she chirped.

"Grr. I hate driving."

"I don't blame you. When are you getting the windows
fixed?"

"I'll drop it off at the shop after work. Boy, it'll be a relief
to go to Willy's instead of practicing."

And that was the way the conversation went, all the way to
school and up to the lab. Cheerful, animated, superficial. She
didn't want to bring up her differences any more than I did,
and I didn't think I could survive another split with her. While
we nattered away about calculus and Willy Preuzer, I was
wondering if this was what being in love was all about: needing somebody so much you were ready to throw away everything else you cared about. Remember that line about "I could
not love thee, dear, so much, loved I not honor more"? It's
bull. If Pat had said: "Hey, Rick, let's go on TV tonight and
show the country how to lift," I would've headed straight
downtown to KST-TV and asked for an audition. But she
didn't, and I was glad.

Gibbs clumped in as usual, and went through his usual
ritual of reading his mail and dropping it in the wastebasket
before starting class. This morning, though, he looked at me
instead of launching into his lecture.

"Stevenson, can you hang around for a minute after class?"

"Yes, sir."

I might've wondered what was up, but we got into some
really interesting math that everybody else was allowed to
handle on the computers. I was eighty-sixed, of course, but I
had fun composing a program to handle the problems Gibbs
gave us, and then let Pat run it on the Apple she was using.
The program didn't work, but it failed in entertaining ways; it
wasn't until class was over that I remembered Gibbs's request.

"How you feeling today?" he asked, once the rest of the
Awkward Squad had drifted off.

"Okay, sir."

"You seemed kind of upset just after the game."

"Well, I sure didn't mean to put anyone in the hospital."

"Suarez told me he was really glad you came to see him."

I goggled at him. It had never occurred to me that Gibbs might be worried about Al Suarez, too. I'd just figured Gibbs was too tough to care about some jerk on the other team.

"His nurse told me he's getting better in a hurry. They checked him out of the hospital this morning."

"Oh, great." Something started to relax inside me, something I hadn't even realized was all knotted up. "Boy, I'm glad to hear that."

"So was I. But that's not what I wanted to talk to you about. Are you free to come to dinner Wednesday?"

"At your place, Mr. Gibbs?"

"Yeah, but you're in luck; I'm not doing the cooking."

"Well, gee—I'd like to, very much. Thank you."

"Good. You can come over with me after Wednesday afternoon practice. Now you better get going or you'll be late for your next class."

The rest of the morning went along pretty much as always, except that in the halls everybody said hello to me and guys punched me in the biceps and said "Way to go!" At lunch, Pat and I went down to the cafeteria and sat with the jocks and kidded each other a lot. Across the room I saw Jason and the Tricycle Rats, including Brad Whatsisface with a big rectangle of gauze taped to his scalp. They didn't pay any attention to us; I was just as glad.

Just as we were finishing, Bobby Gassaway came by. He hadn't been in lab that morning, and I asked him why.

"Putting the finishing touches on my report for tomorrow."

"About time. You still think I'm a little green man from Mars?"

"No. But my dad tells me they chased a couple of UFOs on Saturday."

"A couple of them now. Talk about a waste of taxpayers' money. Gassaway, don't you ever read *The Skeptical Inquirer?*" That's a little magazine that debunks paranormal junk like ESP and UFOs and astral traveling. Gibbs had a lot of copies lying around the lab.

"Sure I read it. They're really biased, though, at least about UFOs. Maybe I'll send them my report after Gibbs gets it."

"Why would they need confetti?" I asked.

"Stevenson, your ass is so smart it almost makes up for the rest of you being so dumb. You'll learn." And he took off after giving me a funny look—almost a smirk. It made me a little uncomfortable, on a day when everybody else had stroked my ego until it developed static cling.

After school I gave Pat and Angela a ride to Angela's place.

"I can't pick you up tomorrow morning," I said. "Brunhilde's going in the shop tonight."

"That's okay. See you at school. The walk'll be good exercise." And she winked at me. What was that supposed to mean?

Willy was all smiles when I walked in. Before I could do a thing, he sat me down in his office and gave me a cup of coffee and sailed into a long, detailed analysis of the game. He'd certainly understood more about it than I had.

"Best game I ever saw Terry High play," he concluded, "and that's saying something. You were fantastic. Listen, you ever think of maybe playing some ball in college, and then turn pro?"

"Pro football. Gee, Willy, I don't think so."

"Aw, come on—think about it at least. You got a real talent for the game, Rick. Talent. I tell you one thing, this Friday they're gonna have a lot of scouts watching you in the stands. Berkeley, UCLA, Stanford, maybe even U of.W."

"Who?"

"University of Washington. You know, up in Seattle?"

"Oh, sure. Well, let's get to work, Willy. I'm costing you money just sitting here."

"Listen, it's a pleasure. I don't get to talk football very often. Boy, that was some game. I get a real bang out of it, you know, see a couple of good teams go to work on each other like that. Everybody evenly matched, none of that big-league pressure for a million bucks a year, just kids playing good ball for the fun of it."

I felt a twitch of guilt and stood up, grabbing a handful of order forms. "Be back with this stuff right away, Willy."

I was glad to be back in the quiet warehouse, doing a familiar job again. Even the tedious parts, like pushing the ladder up and down the aisles when a quick lift would've saved time, were enjoyable. I could almost pretend that the last few weeks hadn't happened, that I was just an ordinary schmo with no problems.

Not lifting turned out to be a good idea, because Willy got bored and came out to keep me company. We talked about the game some more, and business, and what would happen in the next game.

"You better be on your toes," he warned. "Those guys are going to go after you. They're gonna figure you're trouble until they got you on the ground and out of the game."

"Well, I'll try to be careful."

I was already dreading Friday.

After work, I dropped Brunhilde off at the auto body shop and then walked home in the dark. It was over a mile, and I was almost the only pedestrian. Cars whizzed by, and the occasional motorcycle, but no one was walking anywhere. In California, nobody ever does.

Las Estacas Street was just as empty of pedestrians as the rest of town, but at least there weren't many cars. As I reached home I noticed a sedan of some kind, American, parked out in front where Brunhilde usually sat. I glimpsed a couple of people inside, then went on up the walk and let myself inside.

"Actually had to walk home, huh?" Melinda said as I collapsed dramatically into a chair at the kitchen table. "Poor baby."

"It was your basic Third World experience," I wheezed. "You could at least sympathize."

"Hey, I thought you were into hiking."

"That's for the hills, where it's pretty. In town, you go for a walk and you start getting subversive ideas about dynamiting gas stations."

Marcus had been sitting at the entrance to the kitchen, which was as far as he was allowed in until washing up. Suddenly he spun around and took off for the front door, barking in a hysterical baritone. I heaved myself upright and went to see what was up—most likely it was Girl Scouts selling cookies or proselytizers for some religious group asking if we wanted front-row tickets for Armageddon.

Wrong. Holding onto Marcus's collar, I opened the door on two men. One was shortish, stocky, and sandy-haired; the other was tall, rawboned, and dark. Both were wearing cheap slacks and corduroy sport jackets. They were somewhere around thirty, but they looked very solemn.

"Good evening," said the sandy-haired guy. "Are you Richard Stevenson?"

"Yes."

He pulled a little plastic ID card out of the inside pocket of his sport coat, and held it up under the porch light so I could see the little photo of him, in uniform.

"We're from Hotchkiss Air Force Base. Intelligence. Mind if we come in and talk to you for a minute?"

Wow. I'd heard this whole routine before, from the cops who came to nail me for my computer crimes.

"Come on in," I said, yanking Marcus out of the way. "We're just getting dinner ready." Marcus predictably shoved his big beezer into their crotches, and for once I didn't chew him out about it. We all paraded into the kitchen; Melinda looked surprised for a moment, and then her face smoothed out as she, too, remembered the cops.

Sandy-hair identified himself as Mr. Randall; the dark-haired guy was Mr. Borowitz. Despite their reluctance to say much about themselves, they were obviously officers. Melinda invited them to sit down for a bite to eat, which they politely declined.

"We'll only take up a few minutes of your time," Mr. Randall said. "Basically, it boils down to this. Our air traffic controllers have been picking up some, uh, unusual images on radar, usually over Santa Teresa but sometimes up in the hills to the east. They look like some kind of small aircraft, or maybe balloons. They could be a hazard to our aircraft, and we're trying to determine their nature and their origins."

"What's that got to do with us?" Melinda sounded curious, not defensive.

"Well, ma'am," said Mr. Borowitz, "I believe your son Richard is a classmate of the son of one of our air traffic controllers."

"Bobby Gassaway," I explained to Melinda, who rolled her eyes; she'd heard a lot about Bobby.

"That's correct," Mr. Borowitz went on. "Captain Gassaway and some of the other controllers have been assisting Robert Gassaway with a term paper of some kind about UFOs —unidentified flying objects," he added helpfully. "Coincidentally, they started getting these UFOs on radar, which naturally stirred some interest. The appearance of these objects doesn't seem to follow much of a pattern, except that they usually seem to show up late in the evening for an hour or two. We had a couple in daylight over the weekend, though. An aircraft was sent up to investigate."

"Did they see anything?" Melinda asked with a smile. Mr. Borowitz smiled back.

"The pilot did not achieve an optical fix on the objects, no, ma'am, though he did track them on radar." He looked at me as if a hard enough stare would drive me onto my knees, confessing everything; I blinked back at him. "The objects were first observed hovering over the hills in the vicinity of San Miguel Creek State Park. Then they dropped through the overcast and vanished. We understand you go hiking up in that area fairly often, Richard."

"As a matter of fact, I was up there on Saturday," I said. "Among other places. My girlfriend and I were hiking."

"About what time of day?"

"Most of the morning, part of the afternoon."

"When were you at San Miguel Creek?"

"Oh—we must've reached there about nine, nine-fifteen. We hiked up the creek a way. Then we went down 'cause it was getting too wet and cold. We tried a few other trails after that."

"Did you observe anything unusual?" Mr. Borowitz asked.

"No—at least not any flying saucers. It was pretty foggy."

"Isn't this an odd time of year to go hiking?" Mr. Randall wondered.

"Not if you're dressed for it. Most people don't go out, though, so you've got the hills all to yourself."

"Now, Richard," said Mr. Randall, "you seem to have suggested, if we've been accurately informed, you've suggested to Robert Gassaway that these UFOs might be some kind of hoax—and you even predicted when one might be sighted."

"Well, I don't believe in UFOs, so I figured it had to be a hoax. And I was just pulling his leg, predicting when there'd be another one. I was wrong anyway. Have you talked to him much about this?"

"We've spoken with him, yes."

"Well, he's got this bee in his bonnet about UFOs. Even Mr. Gibbs—that's our science teacher—can't get him straight about it. So, well, we tease Bobby a lot about it. He rises to the bait, you know? Anyway, he was going on about flying saucers on his dad's radar, and I just kidded him a little. He thinks I'm behind it."

They both looked a little pained, as if I'd tactlessly brought up some embarrassing subject.

"The suggestion of a hoax of some kind has been mentioned," Mr. Randall agreed. "We understand you got into some trouble last spring over the use you made of your personal computer."

"Yeah. I sure did. Now I can't even use the ones in school, or my mother's, for a year. But what's that got to do with UFOs?"

"Maybe nothing. But the picture we have of you suggests you're a bright young man who's fond of practical jokes. Does it seem to you that something like these UFOs might be a practical joke?"

"Gee, Mr. Randall, I just said so, didn't I? UFOs aren't real, so of course they're a hoax or a joke or whatever. Or else they're just some ordinary thing that's been misinterpreted by Bobby's wishful thinking. At least that's what most of the kids in class think. See, the principle of Occam's razor says you take the simplest explanation that fits all the facts, and you don't complicate your theory with anything unnecessary."

They received this suggestion about as cheerfully as Gassaway himself would have. "Well, maybe you could just give us your opinion," Mr. Randall said.

"Sure."

"If you wanted to pull a UFO hoax—I'm not saying you have, please don't misunderstand me, I'm not saying that at all—I'm saying, if you did want to stage a hoax, how would you go about it?"

"So I got radar images? Wow. Beats me. Maybe with a balloon? I know sometimes people will make little hot-air balloons out of a candle attached to a plastic garbage bag. If it works, you see a light hanging up in the air at night, hardly moving. But would that give you a radar image?"

"Not the kind we've been getting," said Mr. Randall.

"Well, what if the bag was aluminum foil or something with a metallic coating? Or a real hot-air balloon with one of those propane burners underneath it?"

"Maybe. But these objects don't maneuver like a hot-air balloon."

"Well, gee, then I don't know. I can think of stuff like an ultra-light airplane or a glider, but you must've thought of that, too."

They both nodded. Then, as if they'd rehearsed it, they both stood up. Mr. Randall smiled dazzlingly at Melinda, and a little more coolly at me.

"We're really sorry to have disturbed you at this time of day, and we won't keep you any longer. I know it must all sound pretty silly, but when we have to consider the safety of our aircraft, as well as civilian flights, we have to consider every possible hazard, no matter how strange it sounds. You've been very helpful, Richard—Mrs. Stevenson—and I hope if anything else turns up you'll give us a call." He put a business card on the kitchen table. "Thanks again."

I walked them to the front door, with Marcus giving each of them a friendly poke in the rear for old times' sake.

"Gee," I commented as I held the door for them, "I hope the *National Enquirer* doesn't get hold of this story. It'd sound pretty weird."

Mr. Randall smiled insincerely, while Mr. Borowitz looked as if he'd just had an ulcer attack.

"I hope you understand," said Mr. Borowitz, "that this is a very quiet, routine, but confidential investigation. We'd be highly grateful if you didn't mention this to the media—any media."

"I sure won't, Mr. Borowitz. I've got too much respect for

the air force to get it involved in some silly story about UFOs. But I gotta tell you, I'm gonna tease Bobby Gassaway."

They both flashed me embarrassed grins, and walked quickly back to their car. I shut the door and sagged against it for a second before going back into the kitchen. For an improvised performance it hadn't been too bad, but now I was going to have to carry it on with Melinda, whose crap detector was always working fine.

Dinner was on the table, pork chops and rice. Melinda was sitting with her elbows on the table and her fingers laced in front of her face, as if she were about to say grace.

"And what, may I ask, was all *that* about?"

I pulled out a chair and sat down, tucking Mr. Randall's card in my shirt pocket. "I think we've entered . . . deedle-deedle-deedle-deedle . . . the Twilight Zone. Boy, that was *weird*. Melinda, really, it's just Gassaway being an idiot. I pulled his leg a little, and he must've told his dad some fairy tale. It's his dad who sees all these UFOs on radar, so maybe idiocy runs in the family."

Melinda started eating, but she didn't look happy. "It all sounds too crazy to be a mistake, knowing you. And don't roll your eyes at me, buster. I don't have any idea how you could fool radar, but if you could you would."

"But I—"

"I'm not saying you did it, Rick. But after that computer business, I know you're a—a prankster. You get a kick out of doing what you're not supposed to, breaking the rules to see if you can get away with it. Sometimes it's funny, but sometimes it's a drag. And it makes me feel like hell because it means I haven't done such a hot job of raising you to be a caring, ethical kind of person."

What a guilt trip! I put down my fork and folded my arms, even though I knew it made me look like a sulky little boy. Melinda went on for a while longer, and finally ended with: "Do you have anything to say?"

"I sure do. This is a bum rap, Melinda. I have *not* been fooling anybody's radar. I'm not launching any balloons or flying an ultralight or anything. My God, Melinda, I'm too *busy* for pranks."

She sighed and reached across the table to squeeze my hand.

"I'm sorry, Rick. Those jerks just got me upset, that's all."

"Got *you* upset! They didn't exactly sing me to sleep, either."

We got on with dinner, not talking much. Afterward I washed up fast and got on the phone to Pat.

"You got a visit from who?"

"Air force intelligence, if that's not a contradiction in terms. They think I might be hoaxing them about UFOs. Isn't that insane? It's all Bobby Gassaway. That guy has some fantasy life."

"No kidding."

"Listen, you want to come over this evening? I can borrow Melinda's car and come and get you."

"Gee, Rick, I can't. I'm helping Angela with her homework, and I'm not feeling all that great anyway."

"Oh . . . I was just hoping we could talk for a while without the telephone being in the way, you know? Nice and private."

She didn't answer right away. "Yeah, that would be nice. But we'll have to make it tomorrow, okay? I really am stuck for tonight."

"Okay. Well, I better go. Be good. And if you can't be good, be discreet."

"That's an old one. 'Bye."

I hung up and rubbed my palms together nervously. The air force could well be tapping our phone, and I hoped I'd gotten that possibility across to Pat. Her long pause made it seem likely she'd understood, and she hadn't blabbed anything.

The rest of the evening I worked on a couple of essays for English, feeling sorry for myself because I had to use Melinda's old manual portable typewriter; after a computer keyboard, it felt like breaking rocks with a sledgehammer. Melinda went to bed early as usual; I said good night to her and then got ready for bed myself. Events were catching up with me: I was bushed, and just as glad I didn't have Pat around to keep me awake.

With the lights out, I lay in bed and looked at the window. A jet whooshed by overhead; they knew where to find me, though. I wondered if the air force had staked out the house, if they were going to follow me everywhere. Just before terminal paranoia set in, I fell asleep.

13

TUESDAY MORNING. MARCUS woke up and put noseprints all over my face. Sleepily I reached out and scratched his head. Then I remembered what had been going on lately: the trashing of Brunhilde, the jet erupting out of the clouds, Jason nearly getting killed, the air force snooping around, and Pat thinking I was a prime jerk.

Every instinct told me to pull the covers over my head and wait for the world to go away. So I did, but it didn't. Marcus started making ugly remarks about the lack of breakfast. He wanted a dog biscuit, not a master with a nervous breakdown.

"All right, all right," I growled back, and rolled out into the chilly room. A minute later, in jeans and a gray turtleneck, I was on my way downstairs.

I should've stayed in bed. Melinda was making my lunch while I was feeding the dog and rustling up my own breakfast, and we kept getting in each other's way.

"Do you *mind?*" she snapped.

"I'll be right out of your hair," I promised, and grabbed a box of Cheerios.

"I'm sorry to be so crabby," she said a moment later.

"Those men from the base made me nervous. I didn't get much sleep."

"Don't worry. They'll find better things to do when they find out how truly boring I am." Like chase Pat if she keeps on lifting, I added anxiously to myself. I hoped she'd understood the seriousness of the visit from Borowitz and Randall; my call had been pretty circumspect. But I was sure that if they saw any more unexplained blips on their radar, the air force would go into its search-and-destroy mode. They would catch her eventually, and then they'd get me, too, and then they'd bury us in some lab in the desert until we'd taught them how to lift. Or they might decide that lifting was just as dangerous as I'd come to consider it, and then they'd just bury us. I half-wished I'd never let Pat in on the secret. Then I could've laid low (literally) until things calmed down.

Walking to school didn't cheer me up, either. It was a cold, gray day, and I could just imagine how beautiful it must be up on top of the overcast. Every hundred yards or so, I glanced over my shoulder to see if anyone was following me. But this being a typical California street, any pedestrian would have stood out like a rock band in a graveyard. A couple of cars went past me, but neither had Borowitz or Randall in it unless they were wearing hair curlers and make-up.

Crossing the football field toward student parking and the main building, I saw Jason Murphy's Trans Am roll into a slot. It looked pretty bad, but it was running. Jason got out, looking glum, and slouched up the stairs to The Pit. I was far gone in paranoia by now, and considered going the long way around to reach the lab. Then I decided it wasn't worth the trouble, and followed Jason up the stairs.

I hadn't been through The Pit in a while, but not much had changed. The usual hardcore apprentice cancer patients were out there, risking hypothermia as well. They gave me a big welcome, though; I was a football hero now. Jason was standing off to one side with one of the Tricycle Rats—not Brad the bleeder—and they both did me the favor of ignoring me. Still, they made me nervous. Everything made me nervous now.

The lab was like a tomb. Pablo and Ronnie were running their usual boardless chess game, speaking the moves in

undertones. Mason Reeves was staring at the ceiling, his
fingers tapping out the rhythm of some musical piece he was
composing. Eustis Bowson was reading one of Angela Battenbury's romance novels, his eyes wide with astonishment.
He started to laugh, and luckily for him Angela wasn't there;
she's six feet tall, almost as tall as I am, and doesn't like
people to poke fun at her reading habits.

Pat wasn't there, either, and I didn't know whether to be
glad or sad. It would've been great to talk with her, to tell her
how uptight I was getting; but it was also pretty nice not to
have to risk a fight. In the mood I was in, I would've started
shrieking the instant she said anything I disagreed with.

Bobby Gassaway breezed in wearing a new sport shirt—
mostly brown, with sickly yellow stripes—and clean chinos.
He spotted me and came over, taking a plastic binder from
under his arm. His doughy face was wreathed in dimples and
pimples.

"All done," he announced, tapping the binder. "Want to
take a look?"

"Sure," I said casually. I admired my own self-control in
not snatching it out of his hands.

It wasn't all that long, even padded out with his dad's
Polaroid snapshots of radar screens, and a bibliography a page
and a half long. I skimmed it, looking up now and then to see
if Pat had turned up. Gassaway stood fidgeting beside my
chair, waiting for a reaction.

It was a pretty straightforward job, and Bobby had written
it fairly well (with Gibbs as your reader, you watched every
comma). After some fairly well-documented reports of radar
UFO sightings by air traffic controllers elsewhere, he
described the recent rash of local incidents. His quotes from
Papa Gassaway and the other controllers were pretty good;
one of them even got close when he said the radar images
occasionally resembled a parachutist, except that no aircraft
was ever anywhere near them, and of course the images didn't
descend like parachutists. It felt funny to think that guys sitting miles away had actually been watching me all those
times—and watching Pat as well, though Gassaway and his
sources didn't make much fuss over double-image sightings.

Once he got into conjecture over the nature of the UFOs,

Gassaway pulled his punches, sticking closely to the controllers' speculations. These were mostly that the UFOs were some kind of remote-controlled model aircraft, or balloons, or an outright hoax by means unknown. Reading between the lines, I could see Gassaway was torn between just two hypotheses: we were dealing with a subcompact spaceship from some other planet, or Rick Stevenson was continuing his criminal career by conning the U.S. Air Force.

Admiring the neatness of the footnotes, I handed it back.

"*B*-minus," I predicted.

"*B*-minus my ass! That's an *A* paper, hog-jaw."

"I'm betting a buck you don't get better than *B*-minus."

"You're on. But what would *you* give it?"

"About a *C*," I drawled, and ducked, cackling, when he swung at me.

Gibbs's arrival saved me; he came in looking, as usual, like a spell of bad weather.

"Where's Llewellyn?" he demanded, surveying the thin turnout. "And Battenbury?"

"I don't know sir," I volunteered. "They were doing homework together last night. I guess they'll be along soon."

But they weren't.

We noodled through a calculus quiz and some physics, and then Gassaway presented his report. He made it sound better than it was, and even whipped out a couple of transparencies based on his tables, showing the frequency of local UFO sightings over the last year and a half. Boy, it looked obvious: purely random until October, and then the regular late-evening pattern with occasional daylight blips on weekends.

Gibbs listened impassively, and then asked Gassaway a few questions, mostly about his methodology. The answers seemed to satisfy him; he put the report in his briefcase and said he'd have it back in a couple of days. Then we went on to Eustis's genetics report, and that was that.

For a moment I had a crazy, irrational sense of relief: that somehow nobody was going to pay attention to UFOs anymore. Then common sense sank in. Bobby Gassaway might be off my case for the time being, but Mr. Randall and Mr. Borowitz were still out there somewhere, keeping an eye on me.

The only thing I had going for me was the sheer, sweet incredibility of the Effect. Until people actually *saw* me or Pat lifting, they wouldn't believe it. That was a major reason for my giving up lifting, and a major reason for worrying like hell about Pat.

During the break after class I went to the pay phone outside the cafeteria and tried to reach Pat. Morty answered, and said she was sleeping after getting up with a sore throat and a bad headache. I sent my wishes for a quick recovery, while privately enjoying a guilty gladness that she was grounded for a while.

The rest of the day dragged itself out. At three, Melinda picked me up and took me to the body shop. The manager was a lean, dark-haried guy in spotless coveralls who recognized me at once.

"Hi!" he bellowed. "Well, we got 'er all fixed up and ready to go."

I was a little surprised by this hail-fellow-well-met act, since the guy had scarcely noticed me when I'd brought Brunhilde in. And it wasn't just some kind of act to impress Melinda; he paid hardly any attention to her even though she was writing the check to cover the hundred-dollar deductible. Instead, the guy kept looking at me and moaning about how terrible all this auto vandalism was. He made my skin crawl, and it was a relief to get Brunhilde and myself out of his clutches.

At least he'd done a great job on Brunhilde's windows; she looked gorgeous, enough to help me forget I now owed Melinda a hundred bucks I could ill afford on top of my debts to Willy for the biofeedback components. I drove off to work feeling positively cheerful for the first time that day.

The rest of the afternoon was busy but relaxed; Willy had too much work to sit around and talk football, and I was racing up and down the aisles filling orders.

The penny dropped, as they say, not long before I was ready to knock off. I'd been thinking about the body shop manager. He hadn't been looking at me as if he were gay or anything; he'd been nervous, as if he knew something about me. And it occurred to me that my air force fans might have planted a bug in Brunhilde while she was in the shop.

Well, I said I was in terminal paranoia. We carried a good range of anti-bugging scanners, so I grabbed a top-of-the-line model and popped out to the parking area.

Thirty seconds later I was peeling a strip of sticky gray tape off the inside of the right rear fender, and underneath the tape was a pretty little piece of metal and plastic about the size and thickness of two quarters, listing in the catalogs for $79.95 plus tax.

Oh boy. Just because you're paranoid doesn't mean they aren't out to get you.

I hadn't really thought about what I'd do if I found a bug; my first urge was to throw it away. But as Dr. Johnson said, knowing you're going to be hanged in two weeks will powerfully focus your mind. I looked around the twilit parking area, and of course saw nothing. Borowitz and Randall were probably sitting out at Hotchkiss watching a screen that showed a little blip where Brunhilde sat. Chances were that they'd expect the blip to move when I headed for home in a few minutes. If I threw the bug away, they'd know I'd found it and they'd be a lot more careful with the next one. Or else they'd just arrest me for illegally disposing of government property.

Finally—it felt like ages, but probably took about fifteen seconds—I carefully replaced the bug just where I'd found it. As long as they were interested in me, and I was behaving myself, they'd pay less attention to any UFOs that cropped up while my whereabouts were known—so even if Pat went lifting, her chances of getting away with it were better. Even two or three days should be enough, before they got bored or some superior officer got wind of what his ace secret agents were doing. So my job would be to act dumb and carry on like any other red-blooded all-American football hero who'd never even *dreamed* of levitating. At some point, when they'd given up on me, they'd want the bug back, and they'd be annoyed and suspicious all over again if it was missing.

I drove home for dinner, wondering if James Bond had started out like this, and wishing Brunhilde at least had a couple of built-in machine guns.

Just after dinner, I was getting up to phone Pat when she phoned me.

"Hi," she said, sounding tired and stuffy.

"Hi yourself. We all missed you today."

"Missed you, too. I feel awful. All I'm doing is drinking orange juice and sleeping."

"Boy, what a racket. Are you going to be back tomorrow?"

"I don't think so. Angela's got the same thing. We hardly got anything done last night, except blowing our noses."

"Poor baby. I hope you feel better soon. Listen, I collected Gibbs's handouts for you. Want me to bring 'em over tonight? I could go through them with you."

"Ohhh, don't make me even *think* about school. I'm useless. But you're sweet anyway. Can you just hang on to whatever he gives out? And I'll catch up in a couple of days. Unless I get lucky and die."

"Bite your tongue. Sure, I'll save it all."

"What a nice man. Hey, you getting all geared up for the game Friday?"

"Uh, I guess so. We've got a practice tomorrow, and then I'm going to Gibbs's for dinner, so I'll have to call you late."

"Not too late, huh? I'm zonking out around nine-thirty these days."

"Impossible. A night owl like you?"

"Yeah, isn't it sickening?"

I was dying to tell her about Borowitz and Randall and the bug on Brunhilde, but Melinda was right there in the study a few feet away and the phone was likely tapped as well.

"Well, I'll have to come and see you Thursday, right after dinner, unless you get better by then."

"I sure hope I do. Gotta be on my feet for the game."

"I just hope I'm still on my feet *after* the game."

"They'll never catch you."

"Famous last words."

"No, you'll do fine. Listen, I better go now. Call me tomorrow sometime during school, huh?"

"Okay. Every fifteen minutes often enough?"

"Only if Morty lets me keep an extension by my bed, and he won't. 'Bye."

"G'bye."

I hung up the phone and slumped against the wall. For a day that had started out so badly, Tuesday was ending on an upbeat. The skies over Santa Teresa would be empty tonight. I was planning to do some serious homework, and my girlfriend was safely bedridden and out of sight of the junior birdmen.

Now all I had to worry about was the bug on my Bug, my spiralling debts, a physics test tomorrow that would reflect Gibbs at his most creatively fiendish, and on Friday night I would probably get thoroughly tenderized in the game.

"You planning on doing those dishes any time soon?" Melinda yelled from the study.

14

A LITTLE AFTER three o'clock Wednesday afternoon, I was warming up on the edge of the field with the rest of the team. It was a clear, chilly day, the kind that makes you energetic and glad to be alive. I didn't feel either.

The field was occupied for the time being by the school band. Terry High was almost as proud of the band as it was of the football team. The bandmaster was Mr. Fogarty, who looked like a blond Abraham Lincoln; he marched in uniform with the band, all rigged up in a blue-and-gold jacket and blue trousers, strutting like everybody else behind Levon Williams, the drum major. After the forty band members finished their close-order drill, Mr. Fogarty would conduct them through a few pieces from their repertoire: a little Sousa and lots of movie music. The theme from *Star Wars* was popular, and the theme from *Rocky*.

It was a big deal to be in the band, partly because Levon was a great drum major who'd be missed when he graduated next June, and partly because Mr. Fogarty was a good teacher. The band competed all over California; they'd be marching in the Rose Parade on New Year's Day.

Being a cheerleader or a pompom girl was a big deal, too. Every afternoon while we practiced, they practiced, too; since we were drawing big crowds to practices, they were getting really polished. The cheerleaders were three guys and five girls; the guys at least got to wear white trousers, while the girls got goose bumps up and down their long legs because they had just pleated miniskirts and thin blue-and-gold sweaters. But they kept warm by going through routines that were at least as complicated as what we did on the field, and it was prettier to watch.

Still, something about the band and the cheerleaders made me uneasy. When I was in junior high I went through a World War II phase, reading everything I could get my hands on about it, and one item was a history of the early Nazi movement. All that rally stuff of Hitler's, the *Sieg Heil*ing and mass hysteria—that was all cooked up by a German-American with a degree from Harvard. He remembered Ivy League football games and what the cheerleaders could do to whip a crowd into a frenzy, and it worked like a charm for the Nazis. It still worked pretty well in America, too. Hitler's cheerleader, by the way, was named Putzi Hanfstangl, and he got out of Germany a few days before he was scheduled to be pushed out of an airplane.

Doing my jumping jacks and knee bends, I wondered what would have happened if the Nazis had shoved poor old Putzi out the door and then seen him soar off into the clouds. Probably they'd have chased him down to the ground and learned how to lift the whole Wehrmacht.

And the world was still full of guys like Hitler, looking for that little extra advantage over the good guys.

No, I wasn't exactly as cheerful and laid back as a day at the beach. Pat was still sick, and I'd slogged through the day in a state of low-grade anxiety about just about everything except maybe the national deficit. When we trotted out onto the field and everyone started clapping and cheering, I felt like turning around and running like hell. Instead, I scanned the seats, trying to find individuals in the crowd. A lot of students were there, but a lot of adults as well. Melinda was down in the front row, complete with a telephoto lens on her camera. I saw some middle-aged guys in Windbreakers and baseball caps and sunglasses, toting videotape cameras: Gibbs had said they were scouts from San Carlos and Calaveras.

Maybe so, but one of them was sitting right behind my old buddy Mr. Borowitz, and another was cuddling up with Mr. Randall down at the other end of the stands.

Gibbs had already given us the plays he wanted us to practice; now he stood leaning on his cane at the fifty-yard line, ignoring the hundreds of people in the stands behind him.

"Let's go, gentlemen!" he called, and we got to work.

The first play was a simple hand-off and run around right end behind a screen of blockers. I took the ball from Mike Palmer (Jerry Ames was out for at least another week with a sprained ankle) and took off, thinking more about the junior birdmen and their TV cameras than about Sean Quackenbush.

Boy, football was a really different game without lifting! I took so long to get around the line that I began to wish I'd packed a lunch. Sean and the other defenders came after me a little hesitantly, as if they were surprised I was still visible, and then Sean brought me down with a thump.

"Too slow, Stevenson!" Gibbs barked. "Same goes for you tackles. Wake up out there."

So we did it again, with the cheerleaders' chants echoing across the field. I pumped my legs like crazy, and managed to duck past the first tackler, but they still nailed me before I'd crossed the scrimmage line.

Nailed. That doesn't begin to convey the experience of being smashed into by a big guy who then falls on top of you while you crash face-first into the ground and skid for a couple of feet on your chin. It hurts.

After it happened the third time, the noise from the stands changed pitch. A lot of people must have expected to see me racing down the field just like last week. Gibbs called a halt and limped out.

"Stevenson. You feeling okay?"

"Yes, sir. Guess maybe I'm a little stiff after Friday."

"Well, you keep at it. You blockers, you're standing around. You give Stevenson all the protection he needs until he can get clear and do his thing. Understand?" They nodded, and Gibbs turned to the defending squad. "You people, you're letting Stevenson off too easy. The second you see he has the ball, get in there and dump him."

Fear of ever-increasing pain, I discovered, was a pretty fair substitute for lifting. On the next run-through, I took the ball and ran for my life. The blockers did their job, too, and when I broke out no one was close enough to grab me. The spectators clapped and yelled, and the cheerleaders turned cartwheels.

After that, the rest of the practice went a little better. I realized the whole team had fallen into the bad habit of letting me do spectacular stuff while everybody else stood around. Once they did what they were supposed do, a duffer like me had a fighting chance. I even discovered I could still intimidate the opposition; on one play I couldn't outrun Sean, so I ran toward him and threw the timing of his tackle completely off.

Practice finally ended. Gibbs called us around him while the crowd straggled out of the stands.

"You people had me worried for a while," he said. "No matter what anybody says, you cannot play football while asleep. Stevenson, you have got to pick up the pace. You are nothing like as fast as you can be. Palmer, you've got to hand off to Stevenson faster and smoother, and not stand there thinking about it."

He went on with an analysis of our play that took us apart like Lego blocks. I found myself glancing over his shoulder at the air force TV crews, who were casually chatting with Borowitz and Randall as they ambled down the steps, onto the track, and out the exit. Gibbs saw where I was looking and glanced over his shoulder.

"That's another thing. Looks like San Carlos wants to analyze what we're up to. They're going to figure we must be really overrated, and maybe that's okay—*if* we're together on Friday night and playing like last week." Gibbs glared at me. "Speaking of TV, you people are going to be on cable, live, on Friday night. So you better look sharp."

"Yes, sir," we chorused.

"What?"

"YES, SIR!"

"That's right. Okay, go shower."

Once I was dressed, I found a pay phone outside the P.E. office and called Pat. Morty answered, backed up by Twisted Sister or Sibling Giblets.

"She's asleep," Morty yelped over the uproar. "Her fever's gone, but she seems really tired. She's been asleep most of the day. We're hoping she'll be better tomorrow."

"I hope so, too. Tell her to take it easy, and I'll call her tomorrow if she's not in school."

And I went off to the Gibbses' for dinner.

Their house was just a couple of blocks from school, so we walked over together through the twilight. Gibbs talked quietly about the practice—nothing critical, just comments on this guy or that, most of them positive. I walked along beside him, feeling a little odd about going to meet his family when I already knew so much about them from my illegal rummaging through his credit files.

Whatever my preconceptions were, they vanished as Gibbsian reality exploded out the front door to meet us. First came a short, skinny girl in green overalls; behind her was a tall, skinny girl in a white blouse and dressy slacks. They were giggling and squeaking and arguing with each other as they met us on the front walk.

"All right, ladies," Gibbs said cheerfully, "let's settle down and meet our guest. This one"—he hoisted the little one up on his hip, one-handed—"is Diane. Say hello to Rick Stevenson, Diane."

"Hello to Rick Stevenson," she said, and cracked up at her own wit.

"And this is Flora."

"H'lo. Pleased to meet you." She gave me a warm, hard handshake. "You're sure a good football player."

"Thank you."

"We saw you last week. You sure can run."

"Well—"

"Let's get inside," Gibbs suggested. "Diane here is getting entirely too heavy."

The house looked pretty ordinary from the outside, just a plain white stucco with some rose bushes. Inside, though, it was comfortable and welcoming. The floors were gleaming hardwood, and most of the rooms seemed to have floor-to-ceiling wooden bookcases. The furniture in the living room was what you might call Modern Comfortable, stuff that looked good and felt even better when you settled into it and put your feet up. A fire was burning nicely in the fireplace, and the house smelled wonderful from whatever was happening in the kitchen.

Gibbs and I had just sat down when Letitia Gibbs came in from the kitchen. I scrambled to my feet—not because Melinda had taught me manners, but because any conscious male would do so when Letitia Gibbs walked into a room.

"I'm very pleased to meet you," she said. She was a tall woman with broad shoulders and a bright smile; Flora and Diane looked a lot like her. "John's been talking about you, of course, and we all saw you in the game on Friday. You were having a good time out there."

"Oh well," I replied cleverly.

"How did practice go?" she asked her husband.

"Mm, okay. We have some rough spots to iron out."

"Well, just smooth yourselves out by the fire for a few minutes until dinner's ready."

"Can I do anything to help, Mrs. Gibbs?"

"You can help eat, but that's about it."

We made ourselves comfortable by the fire; Flora brought her dad a beer and me a Coke. Then she vanished back into the kitchen while Diane sprawled on the rug in front of the fire, doing homework.

"Here's to Friday," Gibbs said, raising his stein; I lifted my glass in response and smiled weakly.

"What did you think of the practice?" he asked.

"Well, sir, I was kind of disappointed in myself. I was slow."

"You'll pick up again. You know you can do it. Any aches or pains in your legs?"

"Oh, maybe a little, but nothing serious. Guys keep falling on you, you have to expect it."

"Don't be a hero. If you're hurt, we'll pull you out until you're feeling better. We've lost enough people from injuries."

"Believe me, sir, you'll be the first to know. I'm no hero."

"Flora says he is," Diane said slyly.

"You mind your homework," Gibbs told her. The Awkward Squad would have withered under his glare, but Diane just grinned at us.

"You've been having yourself quite a time lately," Gibbs went on. "Are you feeling okay about it all?"

"Well, sir, I'm busier than I've ever been in my life."

"I believe it. You getting enough sleep?"

"Oh, sure. After a practice like today, I don't have any trouble getting to sleep. Just trouble waking up."

"Well, we'll take it easier on you tomorrow. I want you good and rested for Friday. What else have you been up to?"

I nearly twitched, as if he'd revealed my guilty secret. "Gee, I don't know. Hiking some. Reading a lot. Working, of course. I haven't had an electronics project since the biofeedback device."

"You're not jamming the radar out at the base?" Gibbs smiled.

"No, sir. Bobby Gassaway may think I am, though."

"I know. It's all over his report. Did you know the air force has been asking questions about you?"

"Well, they've been asking me, so I guess it figures they'd be asking other people. Did they talk to you, sir? Mr. Borowitz and Mr. Randall?"

"Those are the names, all right. They came round to see me a couple of nights ago. I couldn't tell them much."

"They were in the stands this afternoon."

"I saw them. And the cameramen they had with them."

"I thought you said they were scouts from San Carlos."

"I saw the cameras first. Built my hypothesis on them. Then I saw the two gentlemen, so I had to revise the hypothesis. I think it's pretty robust now. They're really interested in you, Stevenson."

"Well, sir, I think it's all pretty silly when it isn't being kind of scary. If they think I can fool their radar, they're crazy."

"I agree. Any hypothesis on why this should be happening to you?"

"No sir, except coincidence."

Gibbs shifted his weight in his easy chair and steepled his

fingers. "Coincidence. Coincidence of what?"

"Oh, of, you know, Bobby Gassaway's thing about UFOs and the sightings." That had been close; I'd been thinking, of course, of the coincidence of the sightings and my newly acquired abilities. My answer didn't completely make sense, but Gibbs let it pass with a frown.

"And you're not involved with any project that might, for instance, accidentally interfere with radar."

"Sir, if I was I'd sell it to the air force for sixty million dollars, not try to hide it from them."

Gibbs smiled. "And Pat Llewellyn's not using any electronic devices, either, I take it?"

"No, sir. I'd know if she was."

"You two seem to have hit it off pretty well."

"I guess so. She's a great girl."

"She's not stupid. By the way, how's she feeling?"

"Not too great, I guess. I called her just before we left school, and she's been sleeping most of the time."

"Next time you talk, tell her I asked after her."

"Yes, sir."

"She's changed a lot since she came to Terry High."

"I guess so."

"Not quite so prickly."

"Not like that first day, no, sir."

We chuckled a little, and Flora called us in for dinner.

The family and I sat down in the dining room while I wondered what Gibbs was after. He must be really mystified by having air force intelligence agents dropping in on him, and asking questions about his weird and wonderful new running back.

My worries were soon buried under an avalanche of first-rate food: ham, baked potatoes, broccoli, home-baked rolls, and a small mountain of tossed salad. The conversation was easy and domestic, with the girls chiming in whenever they liked but not interrupting. I thought I could have gone on eating all night, but Letitia finished me off with a huge slab of apple pie smothered in vanilla ice cream. Two more bites and I'd have slid into a catatonic trance; as it was, I just barely managed to waddle back into the living room with Gibbs.

Flora and Diane cleared the table and filled the dishwasher, while Letitia joined us with a pot of coffee.

"I hear you're a science-fiction reader," she said, pouring me a cup. "What are you reading these days?"

"Mm, well, Frank Herbert," I said, a little surprised. "And some old Heinlein."

"Hard-science stuff," she said with a smile. "I like Le Guin better."

"Letitia is a big fan," Gibbs said dryly. "I can take it or leave it."

"Mostly leave it. John has no imagination."

"I have too much imagination. With most of that stuff, you can see all the holes in the science and that spoils it for me."

"He must be really boring to have as a teacher," Letitia said sympathetically.

"Oh, not exactly," I answered with a nervous smile. But the turn in the conversation gave me an idea. "Actually, I've been working on a science-fiction story."

Gibbs's eyebrow rose. "First I've heard of it."

"What's it about?" Letitia asked. Flattered silly by so much attention from a beautiful woman, I gathered my wits for a few seconds.

"It's about a guy who discovers a, a new source of energy. It's cheap, it's really efficient, it doesn't pollute, and uh, just a matchbox full of it will run a car for a lifetime."

Gibbs looked just the way he did in class when you tried out a wrong answer on him. "What's the source of the energy?"

"He, uh, doesn't know. He only know that when he puts this little gadget together, it works. He can heat his home, run his lights, and it's like something for nothing."

"Very nice. What else?"

"Uh, well, the trouble is, he's afraid it might be misused if he announces it. Somebody might build bombs out of it, and it's so cheap and easy that almost anybody could do it. Besides, he's afraid the army or the energy corporations will go after him to get the secret. So he decides to bury the whole idea."

"That's the whole story?" Gibbs looked disappointed.

"Wait. First, what kind of person is your hero? A scientist?"

"Sort of, uh, an amateur or a student. I don't know yet for sure."

"But he's figured out this new source of power."

"Stumbled on it, really."

"Can he work out the implications?"

"Sir?"

"Can he work out the physics, the chemistry of this new energy source? How does it fit into what's known already?"

"I don't know."

"That's what bothers me about this kind of writing. You never get to find out what's really interesting. Like they tell you the hero uses a space warp to get somewhere, and all he does when he gets there is shoot holes in little green men. I want to know about that space warp, not about green men. Now, if you've got this new source of energy, and you're not just telling fairy tales, it's got to have a physics and chemistry and a whole set of properties. The way you describe it makes it sound like Aladdin's lamp."

"Okay, sir. Let's say it's antigravity, and it's a property of matter that we haven't even suspected yet, like Aristotle never suspected electromagnetism. You can get work out of gravity, and you can get work out of antigravity."

"And why haven't we discovered it yet?"

"Gee, do I have to explain everything, Mr. Gibbs? I mean, in this kind of story the gimmick is just a way to have fun."

"Right, so do a good job of it."

"Okay. Let's say it's a quantum-physics phenomenon, something that's observer-dependent. Just like quantum physics seems to need an observer before anything happens, this antigravity thing needs somebody to expect it to happen. And then it does."

Gibbs looked bleak. "Unpersuasive, Stevenson."

"Well, sir, Aristotle could sit in this room for years and never touch the button that turns on your stereo. And if I told him he could get music out of the air by doing something as arbitrary as pressing a button on a metal box, he'd be unpersuaded, too. And since he wasn't big on experiment, he'd write me off as a nut case and never press the button."

"Arguments by analogy are always pretty shaky. Well, now

work it out. What happens if your hero stops thinking about his antigravity gadget? Does it stop working?"

"I guess so."

"So if he's asleep, or distracted, it stops?"

"Uh-huh."

Gibbs shook his head. "I don't buy it. A phenomenon that needs somebody thinking about it—it's just another name for magic."

"Or another name for a whole range of phenomena that occur only in the presence of a field of consciousness."

"More gobbledygook. A lot of psychologists like to argue that consciousness itself doesn't exist. But work on it, Stevenson. If you can develop the details it might be fun."

"Tell me what you think about the plot, sir. D'you think the hero should keep his discovery a secret?"

"It's not exactly a new plot in science fiction, is it? *Could* he keep it a secret? What's to keep somebody else from discovering it?"

"Oh, let's say you have to be in this special state of mind to blend yourself into the consciousness field."

Gibbs sat back, his bad leg stretched out to the fire, and drank his coffee. "Let's consider some of the consequences of this mind-powered antigravity before you get yourself all tied up in knots. A source of power. Controlled mentally. Anybody else can learn to use it, too, right?"

"Yes, sir. Once they know how."

"And then you can make your car run without gas, that kind of thing?"

"Uh-huh."

"You say good-bye to the oil industry, all right. And nuclear power, and hydro power. No more coal mines, except maybe to supply the chemical industry. You need a way to transmit this power?"

"No, sir. It's everywhere; you just have to tap into it."

"Like Nikola Tesla turning the whole planet into a battery. It's all too easy. You ought to give this gadget some drawbacks, like any other energy source. Otherwise you end up with some half-baked Utopia."

"That's easy, sir. It makes a terrific weapon, like I said. So you could blow things up really easily. It gives people plenty of mobility, so armies or refugees or anybody could go almost anywhere they felt like."

Gibbs snorted. "With so much power, who needs mobility? Who's going to bother to stay in an army?"

"So we're looking at social collapse," I said. "Something like anarchy."

"Dictatorships think *we're* something like anarchy, letting people do what they damn well please. Other people always look disgraceful when they have more freedom than you do."

"Maybe you wouldn't have full-size armies," I countered, "but even two or three guys could pack a wallop. Right now, we get some psycho maybe once or twice a year, a guy with a gun complex who murders twenty-five people in a restaurant or something. What if the psycho had this gadget, and he could blow up a small town?"

Gibbs didn't answer for a moment. Then he said: "If we thought that was too high a price to pay for the gadget, we'd find a way to discourage people from blowing up towns. Or we might find that losing a couple of towns a year was just a nuisance compared to the benefits."

"Oh, John!" Letitia sighed. I could see that being Mrs. Gibbs wasn't always fun.

"We kill sixty thousand people a year on the highways because that seems to be an acceptable price for the convenience of automobiles. If we made cars safe, they might be too expensive to be convenient. Why should we consider this gadget any differently?"

"If they all got killed in one town, sir, on one day, we might try to do something about it."

"Touché," Letitia said. "I'd love to read your story, Rick, when you get it finished."

I shook my head. "After all this, ma'am, I don't know if I should even get started on it. I hadn't worked out all the implications."

"We never do," said Gibbs.

"You ought to think about your hero," Letitia said. "Make him a certain kind of person, and the decision should come out of his personality."

"Science fiction isn't interested in character and personality," Gibbs announced. He looked at the fire for a moment.

"Might be interesting, though, if you made your hero a guy who can't stand secrets. A regular busybody who wants to find out everything, and then *he's* got a secret he's afraid to let out."

"That's an idea," I agreed, feeling my skin prickle. "Maybe you ought to write the story, Mr. Gibbs."

"Ha! That's one thing I can't do. No, it's your story, you work it out."

It could drive you wild, the way Gibbs refused to do your thinking for you. I was glad when he changed the subject.

"I'm going to leave you alone a little in practice tomorrow. Today you looked like you were trying too hard to live up to your image. Like the centipede thinking about how to walk. Just relax and be part of the team."

"I'll sure try, sir."

"There you go again. *Don't* try. Just do what you're supposed to do. We'll work on plays that don't put all the pressure on you, and then when it's your turn to carry the ball it won't be any big thing. Okay?"

"Okay."

"Good."

We chatted about the team, and school, and then it was time to leave. The girls popped out in their pajamas to say good-bye, and Letitia told me to come back again soon. Gibbs just stood there, smiling and looking inscrutable as I thanked everyone in sight and left.

It was a cold, dry night, with a breeze that stung my eyes but tasted good. I walked back toward the school, where Brunhilde was parked. Gibbs's reaction to my phony story had given me a lot to think about. He knew I was up to something; he didn't know what it was, but he wasn't going to pry it out of me and tell me what to do about it. He was treating me like an adult with a mind of my own, and it was driving me bananas.

As I unlocked Brunhilde a motion flickered in the corner of my eye. I glanced down the street and saw someone, just a shadowy figure, pause by a tree half a block away and then turn casually away.

Great. They only had to tail me while I was away from the bug taped to Brunhilde's bumper. A very thoughtful saving of taxpayers' dollars. Still, it made me uncomfortable and annoyed to think that they were still following me when I was being totally straight and boring.

The evening wasn't that old, so I drove over to Pat's. As usual, the house stereo was playing the rock version of the Battle of Stalingrad, in Dolby. Morty let me in with a big hello, the only kind that was audible over the noise, and told me Pat was doing homework down in the basement rec room. I went downstairs and found her there—with Angela Battenbury.

"How are you guys feeling?" I asked as I settled into one of the ratty armchairs. What a contrast from the Gibbses' living room! Cheap panelling, a couple of couches and chairs, a broken TV set in the corner. Pat and Angela were sitting at a card table with physics and chemistry texts piled up in front of them.

"I think we're better," Pat said. "But far from great."

She was right. Both of them looked a little haggard—dark circles under their eyes, pasty complexions, their hair looking ratty and neglected.

"What have we missed in school?" Angela asked.

"Judging from what you're working on, not much. You look like you're ahead of me in physics. It's been a really dull week."

"I hear you were having trouble in practice," Pat said.

"Boy, your spies are everywhere."

"Nobody expects the Spanish Inquisition," Pat hissed. "They say you volunteered to be a tackling dummy."

"Something like that. Gibbs thinks I'm feeling the pressure too much."

"I believe it. You can really get uptight about that jock stuff."

"What's that supposed to mean?" I snapped. "Think I like getting nailed? Well, I don't."

"See, that's just what I mean. I make one little comment and you get all upset."

"How come when a girl gets upset she's in touch with her feelings, and when a guy gets upset he's a jerk?" I asked.

"Beats the hell out of me," Pat confessed. "Maybe jerkiness is close under the male surface."

"When you're shallow," said Angela, "everything is close under the surface."

"I liked you guys better when you were too sick to talk," I said. "I could get this kind of flak at home from Melinda. No, actually I'm glad you're so obnoxious. It shows you really are getting well. Want a ride to school tomorrow?" I asked Pat.

"If I go. Morty thinks I ought to stay home another day. He says it's better than collapsing halfway through school and staying out for another week."

"Well, I'll call just before I leave. I've missed you, y'know."

"Is that why you're already getting up to go?"

"I'm bushed. Playing football is a great way to learn how to fall asleep early. You guys get some sleep, too."

"Don't worry," Angela laughed hoarsely. "We've been sleeping all day. Sleeping our lives away."

They walked me back upstairs; Angela turned down my offer of a lift home, saying her dad was coming by for her in a few minutes. I gave Pat a little kiss on the cheek as I stepped out the door, and she wrapped her arms around my neck and hugged me.

"Unclean, unclean!" she moaned, and kissed me hard. "Why should you be healthy when we're sick, sick, sick?"

"Serve you right if I come down with the galloping crud in the middle of the game Friday night."

"Isn't that what they call the San Carlos team—the Galloping Crud?"

"The crud will be me if I don't get home and rest up. 'Bye. 'Bye, Angela." Angela grinned at me, eye to eye; she really was tall.

As I got back into Brunhilde, I saw somebody get into a parked car down the street, heard him turn on his engine, and watched him sit there, idling. When I pulled away from the curb, he followed me home. Maybe they didn't trust the bug after all.

I wished Pat had been alone. I really wanted to talk to her, talk with her, share my confused feelings about everything that was going on. Instead I spent the end of the evening up in my room, explaining matters to Marcus. At least he listened and didn't give me a lot of snide comebacks.

15

"How's PAT?" MELINDA asked from the study. I lifted my muzzle out of a bowl of Cheerios and grunted; the phone rang.

"Aha," I said. "Maybe that's herself."

"Hi," said herself. "Can I bum a ride to school, please?"

"School? School? Oh—I recognize your voice. You're Pat Llewellyn! Gee, Pat, don't you realize what's happened? You've been in a coma for twelve years. I don't go to school any more. In fact, after I graduated from Yale I set up my own computer company and made a hundred million dollars before I was twenty-five. But I'll tell you what—just for old times' sake I'll send one of the company chauffeurs over, and he'll take you to school."

"If it's got to be a chauffeur, it better be a big Mercedes."

"He'll be there in ten minutes."

". . . You know, for a second you really had me going there."

"Now you're putting *me* on. See you soon."

Melinda tilted back in her ergonomic chair so she could see me in the kitchen.

"You know something, Rick? You're *weird*."

* * *

Pat was waiting out on the sidewalk, her bookbag slung over one shoulder. She was leaning against her cane, and her breath made little puffs of white in the early morning sunshine.

"Hi, stranger." I leaned over and kissed her as she got in. "Ooh, cold."

"Ooh, hot. Hi."

"How you feeling?"

"Tired, but I guess I'll live."

"Say that again after you see what Gibbs has been doing to us all week. If you know what's good for you, you'll have a relapse."

"Sounds good. Hey, I missed you."

"I missed you, too. This has been a hairy week." I told her about Mr. Borowitz and Mr. Randall, which she thought was hysterical, but I didn't tell her about the bug they'd planted behind Brunhilde's bumper.

"Also," I added in a bid for pity, "I'm getting the everloving tar knocked out of me in practice."

"No lifting, huh?"

"Just muscle power."

"That's awful," she said with a grin. "Can I see your bruises?"

"Why should I cheer you up? It's going to be a massacre tomorrow. I ought to call in and say you've infected me. Then Gibbs wouldn't waste his time trying to get me to perform."

"Or you could perform."

"With Gassaway's friends up in the stands, videotaping me? Forget it. I just want to sneak back into the underbrush."

"Boy, what a sissy."

"When are you gonna learn the difference between sissy and paranoid?"

Just then I had a genuinely paranoid insight: maybe they'd put a microphone inside the car. What had we said? Anything incriminating? Pat had said something about lifting, something about performing. Would that be enough to give us away? I got goose pimples.

"Let's drop the subject for now, huh?"

"Okay, boss."

For the rest of the ride she was cheerful and relaxed, chatting about what she'd have to do to catch up with the Awkward Squad. I felt a little easier, knowing that she wasn't going to give me a hard time and argue about anything.

We got to school, and my heart sank again. The whole place had been decked out with banners for tomorrow's game: "Sink the Buccaneers," "Saints Rule OK," all that great school-spirit stuff. The walls were plastered with notices about a pep rally at lunchtime today. Terry High was going into its yearly end-of-season frenzy, and I could just imagine how popular I was going to be on Saturday morning after the Buccaneers martyred the Saints. With luck I'd be unconscious in an oxygen tent.

It was even getting to Gibbs, I think. He wasn't happy to see that Eustis Bowson and Mason Reeves were absent—that put Mason deep in the dungpile, because he'd been scheduled to present his project. Angela was back, but not looking great, and she could hardly speak. Pablo and Ronnie went on playing chess as always, but for once Gibbs was annoyed with it and ordered them to quit and pay attention.

"But we always do pay attention, Mr. Gibbs," Pablo protested gently. It was true.

"Pay more," Gibbs growled, and the morning was off to a lurching start. It went on like that, with Gibbs snapping at us while we sat there doing our brain-death imitation. After an hour or so, Angela raised her hand.

"Please, Mr. Gibbs," she whispered hoarsely, "may I be excused? I'm afraid I'm not as well as I thought I was."

"Go talk to the nurse, Battenbury. If she thinks you ought to go home, you may. Otherwise, take it easy down there until lunch."

I glanced worriedly at Pat. "How are you feeling?'

"Not that bad, anyway."

We were down to just a handful of people, and we lost critical mass. Gibbs knew it, and put us to work on individual reading assignments for the rest of the morning.

At lunchtime, the central quad was a seething mass of crazy people. The band was blasting away with, of course, "When the Saints Go Marching In." The cheerleaders and pompom girls were up on the sundial, a big circular tiled platform in the middle of the quad, goading everyone into mass hysteria. One of the male cheerleaders (I could never tell them apart—they were all blond and clean-cut and smiled too much) was getting everyone to practice their wave, and with everyone sitting down and standing up in sequence around the quad, the effect was a little nauseating.

I would have preferred staying in the lab for lunch, or even hanging out in the john with Jason Murphy and the Tricycle Rats, but of course I had to be at the rally. The cheerleader quit making everybody wave, and began to introduce the team, calling them up onto the sundial to stand in a self-conscious cluster. When he called my name, everybody screamed and clapped and whistled.

Feeling like a jerk, I stepped up on the sundial and waved, which only made things worse. The cheerleaders were right next to me, but I couldn't hear what they were saying over the uproar. I looked around; Pat was where I'd left her, off at the edge of the quad where she wouldn't be shoved and her cane wouldn't get in anybody's way. She grinned and blew me a kiss.

Over on the other side of the quad were Gibbs and Mr. Gordon, each standing with his arms folded; I had the uncomfortable feeling that they were looking only at me. And not far away from them was Bobby Gassaway, with an expensive-looking Nikon 35mm, snapping pictures of the team. That surprised me; he'd never been much of a football fan, still less the kind of guy who takes pictures at pep rallies. Once again, paranoia explained it: the fink must be standing in for Mr. Borowitz and Mr. Randall. They would've attracted a lot of unwelcome attention on the school grounds during class time. I was tempted to do a quick lift while Gassaway was between exposures, and then let him explain to his air force friends why he hadn't caught me doing it on film.

Instead, I just stood there and grinned like somebody with a fresh lobotomy, while the band played and cheerleaders did war dances and everybody had a good time except me.

Finally it was all over except for Mr. Gordon's speech. He struggled through the crowd, hopped up on the platform, and shook everybody's hand. His red hair stood out in all directions from his freckled scalp.

"We've got a great team, people," Mr. Gordon shouted into a microphone while the loudspeakers sent echoes around the quad. "Tomorrow night we're going to show San Carlos how it's done, and then we're going to beat Calaveras and take the championship again. You know how we're going to do it, people?"

"How?" everybody yelled on cue.

"We've got the coach," Mr. Gordon yelled, and the bass drummer thumped his drum for punctuation. "We've got the team." Everybody was chanting along now. "We've got the pep. We've got the steam." Thumpety-thump, while everybody screamed and the cheerleaders bounced up and down in their little pleated skirts.

"And we've got Rick Stevenson!" Mr. Gordon added, waving toward me. Over the uproar, he shouted, "Rick's going to have an even better game than he did last week, right, Rick?"

I grinned some more and shrugged and wished I'd never decided to show off against Jason in that stupid basketball game.

Here is one good thing about having a morbid imagination: you can imagine so many horrible things that reality, no matter how bad it may be, is usually a pleasant surprise by comparison. That was how it was with the practice that afternoon.

Gibbs kept his promise to ease up on me. We did a lot of passing plays, and I mostly hung around and kept guys from sacking Wes. The crowd in the stands was pretty big, but I didn't see Mr. Borowitz or Mr. Randall or even Gassaway. Once or twice, some kids tried to get a chant going—"We want Rick," all that—but it didn't work. People seemed happy just watching a good high-school ball team doing its thing.

After a while I did start carrying the ball, and it wasn't as bad as I'd expected it would be. I was moving fairly fast, and my blockers kept pace with me, so I managed to gain some ground most of the time. Once, though, I got confused and Sean Quackenbush bashed into me so hard I lost my breath. Sitting there on the cold grass, trying to breathe, I remembered how Jason had looked after I'd slammed into him. It was almost worth it to know exactly how lousy he must have felt.

Apart from that, though, the practice was okay. I positively bounced into the locker room, thinking that maybe I was going to get through the game alive, and not cost us the game in the process. Nobody gave me any flak about being slow, and Gibbs looked positively cheerful. He could do both sides of the good cop–bad cop routine, and make you glad he'd run you silly. Now he was moving around the locker room, talking to guys in a quiet, personal way, as if each guy was the key element in his master plan, and we all glowed in the dark when he moved on.

Showered and cheerful, I walked out and found Pat waiting for me.

"Hi," I said. "What are you reading?"

"One of Angela's romances. In a dopey kind of way, it's pretty good."

"Angela is a bad influence on you."

"Angela is a good person."

"Hey, sure. I *like* her. It was just a remark, okay? Can I give you a lift home or anything?"

"How about Hillside Park?"

"Your wish is my command."

It was a gorgeous evening, with the sun low in the sky and the western horizon dotted with clouds turning pink and black. Off to the east, the Sierras were white and gold and purple; in between, the whole valley stretched out below us, close enough to touch in the clear air. A jet lifted from Hotchkiss and howled off through the empty sky toward the north, its underside glinting in the sunset.

"You looked pretty good out there today," Pat said as we walked along the edge of the bluff, right where we'd been that first day she'd come to school.

"I'm a shadow of my former self." We turned away through a grove of pines to Duck Lake. It was really just a pond, but it did attract a lot of ducks. At this time of year most of them were transients from up north, some of them planning to head farther south and some staying put. They were cruising around the reeds and lily pads, looking for supper.

"You're not going to lift in the game, huh?"

"I'm not lifting at all just now, like I told you. Too dangerous. How about you?"

"I'm being careful."

"That's what people say just before they get pregnant."

She gave me a rap on the knee with her cane, but her heart wasn't in it; I could still walk.

"I'm being careful, I said. But I think this is all a big drag, with you on the ground all the time."

"Hey, I know. I know. But what else can I do, Pat? It's just too dangerous with all these weird people watching me. I even talked to Gibbs about it—"

"You told him?" she gasped.

"Of course not, you airhead. I told him I was working on a science-fiction story."

"Ooh. Clever."

"As a matter of fact, it was. But all he did was tell me to work out the story the way I thought it ought to go, and that's what I'm doing."

"Well, I think you're really wrong, and it makes me mad. I still have to lug this stupid brace around, and walk really slow when I could just lift wherever I wanted to go. And millions of people like me could do the same, instead of rotting in wheelchairs or on crutches."

"Pat, we've gone over all this before. For Pete's sake, all I'm doing is buying time, trying to see where problems might turn up. We've only known about this for a few weeks, right? My gosh, they don't even bring out a new brand of *tooth*paste that fast. They do tests. They look for trouble."

"Trouble is just what you're not looking for."

"Aw, come on."

"No, *you* come on. You've been twisting yourself into knots about this. You're the guy who can't stand secrets, and you're sitting on the biggest one in the world. If it was Gassaway who could lift, and you got even a hint of it, you'd never quit until you learned all about it."

This was close enough to what Gibbs had said that it made me sore. I stopped short and turned to Pat. In the twilight, her face was just a pale blur.

"Look. Lifting was *my* discovery. If something goes wrong

with it, it's my fault. I'm responsible."

"Your discovery. Does that mean it's your property? Am I supposed to pay you a royalty every time I lift? Do you charge by the mile?"

She turned away from me, so quickly and fluidly that I knew she was lifting, and I felt a burst of envy. Then she glided away from me, toward the edge of the lake a few feet away.

"What are you *do*ing?" I hissed. No one else was in sight, but I was taking no chances.

"Walking on water. Want to make something out of it?"

And there she was, standing just on the surface of the lake and moving slowly out into the darkening lake.

"Pat, for heaven's sake—please!"

The next thing I knew, I'd followed her, without lifting, and I was in the lake up to my crotch.

It was cold. It was truly cold. I yelped and she turned and saw me grabbing for her ankle, trying to drag her down.

"You turkey!" Then she took my hand in hers and hoisted me out of the water and back onto the trail. I shuddered and started doing a little dance in my squelchy running shoes. "What'd you do that for?"

"What'd *you* do that for?" I snapped back. "Somebody could've seen you."

"Boy, are you ever far, far gone. It's almost pitch black already, nobody else is around anyway, and you're trying to avoid attention by jumping in the lake and screaming and scaring all the ducks. Now you have to drive us home dripping wet."

"It's okay. I'll just tell Melinda I accidentally fell in."

"No, tell her you did it on purpose. Come on."

We went back down the trail. It was farther to the parking lot than I'd remembered, and I was turning blue by the time we got there.

"Get out of those pants," Pat ordered.

"Are you nuts?"

"You're nuts if you stay in them. Go on, it's too dark to see anything anyway."

Keeping Brunhilde between me and the nearest street light,

I peeled my clammy jeans off and got a scuzzy blanket out of the back seat. Marcus used it when he went for rides with me, and it smelled of wet dog. Even so, it felt great to be wearing something warm and dry. I wrapped it around myself like a sarong, and slid behind the wheel. My feet were freezing in wet runners, but I figured we'd be home before frostbite set in.

Pat got in beside me, still giggling, and I started the car. We pulled out of the lot, and just up the street I saw a sedan parked with its lights off. Brunhilde's lights swept across it, and I recognized the two men inside.

"It's Mr. Borowitz and Mr. Randall," I said.

"The air force guys?"

"Yeah. Now doesn't that show you something?" I demanded. "This isn't just some paranoid pipe dream. I've got real people following me."

"I think it's a riot."

I growled and snarled all the way down the hill and past the school, watching the sedan's headlights in my rearview mirror. It was all too weird: a clean-living high-school student, driving through a normal California city wearing a dog blanket while being followed by military spies, and the normal guy's crazy girl friend is about to wet her pants laughing.

"Don't talk about anything sensitive," I muttered through my chattering teeth as we slowed for a red light. "They may have put a microphone in the car."

"Oh gee, I hope so!"

We halted at the intersection, and the sedan stopped right behind us. Pat glanced over her shoulder, and then suddenly got out of the car.

"Hey," I croaked, and watched her limp back to the sedan. I rolled down the window to yell at her to come back, and heard her tell them:

"There's a man in that car, and he doesn't have any pants on."

For one horrible moment I seriously thought about leaving her there. Then I decided she'd just lift after me, and that would be game over. Instead, I waited for her to come back. She climbed in and shut the door just as the light turned green.

"Oh—oh—you should've seen their faces, Rick! Oh, they looked just like you!" And she just about expired right there in my car.

"Don't you dare tell Melinda," I commanded her, but I'm not sure she could hear me over her own laughter.

16

MELINDA THOUGHT IT was funny, too. She didn't even much care how I'd gotten wet; the sight of me in Marcus's blanket threw her into delighted hysterics. With all the dignity I could muster, I marched upstairs and changed into dry pants and shoes. Then I came downstairs to find hot chocolate waiting for me.

"I didn't think you could make hot chocolate and laugh that hard at the same time," I grunted.

"God knows it isn't easy," Melinda said, and that set the two of them off again.

Finally I drove Pat home. We didn't say much, mostly because I was a little sulky. She gave me a friendly little kiss when I parked in front of her place.

"Get some sleep, No-Pants," she said, and slid out of the car before I could slug her.

The rest of the night was long and bad. The jets kept booming overhead, and Marcus kept scratching himself, and I kept waking up every few minutes to see if Friday morning had finally arrived. When it did, I was too groggy to care.

A breakfast that could have fed the whole team was set out

for me on the kitchen table, and Melinda had deserted her study to keep me company. "Rah rah sis boom bah," she greeted me.

"Give me a break," I groaned, and started eating to forget my troubles.

It was a clear, cold morning, with the sun shining on the frost-tipped grass. The weather would be perfect for the game. Too bad; in pouring rain I could have pretended to slip and pull a tendon or something. I ran through various scenarios that would get me out of the game early and uninjured. None of them seemed very likely, but they kept me from facing reality until breakfast was all gone and Pat was on the phone, asking for a ride.

"Sure," I said. "But if I turn up in a dirty raincoat with nothing underneath it, it'll be all your fault."

"Beggars can't be choosers," she chirped, and hung up.

I went out to Brunhilde and went over her whole interior, looking for a microphone. Nothing. I checked underneath. Nothing. The bug behind the fender was still there. Somehow I didn't think it could pick up a conversation on the other side of a VW engine. That made me feel a little better.

Pat looked tired when I came by, but she gave me a smile and a kiss as she got in.

"Hi. All set for the game?"

"Don't talk to me about the game. I'm sick to my stomach thinking about it."

"You sure you aren't making extra trouble for yourself by all this?"

"Very sure."

"Okay. I won't say anything more about it. All right?"

I looked at her, a little surprised. "Sure. Thanks. You change your mind about it or something?"

"I just figure you've got enough to worry about without me nagging at you. Let's just get through the day."

"Hear, hear." I patted her hand, feeling grateful.

Terry High was even more wrought up than the day before. More banners, more blue-and-gold crepe streamers, more posters promising death to San Carlos, more people socking me in the arm and wishing me luck. I felt like one of the sacrificial victims the Aztecs used to pamper for a year before cutting them open.

Eustis and Mason were absent, which made Gibbs a little annoyed with all of us. He was used to good attendance, and this week a lot of us had been out with one thing or another. Maybe he was edgy about the game also; anyway, he was a bit testy until we got into a discussion of quantum weirdness and everybody started having a good time. I don't pretend to understand it all, but the idea of subatomic particles popping into existence out of nowhere, and not behaving like anything until someone's watching them, is nothing but fun to people like the Awkward Squad. For us, the macroscopic world is already pretty strange, so weirdness on the quantum level seems perfectly natural.

Around ten o'clock I went to the john and there, in his natural habitat, was Jason Murphy. He was leaning against the frosted glass of the window, looking out through a slightly open pane at the football field. When I came in, he glanced over his shoulder at me and went back to smoking and staring.

"You gonna be a big hero tonight," he remarked.

"Well, we'll see."

"I been watchin' you in practice. You're holdin' back. Real smart."

I finished my business and went to wash my hands. It was strange having an actual conversation with Jason—like talking to a doorknob and getting answers.

"What d'you mean, holding back?"

"You seen everybody watchin' you in the stands. Guys with TV cameras. Lotta money gonna ride on the game. They see you gettin' your ass whipped, they're gonna bet on San Carlos. Figure you just had a lucky night last week, 'cause you sure don't look like anything now."

"You think I'm just holding back, huh?"

"Man, I played you, remember? You can't fool me. Nearly broke my neck. And you busted up those other guys, and even Quackenbush. So you figure you overdid it, huh, and you go easy all week. Tonight you do your thing, and San Carlos is dogmeat."

"Did you bet on me?"

He grinned through a mouthful of smoke. "Two hundred, at three to one."

"You're going to lose, Jason."

Jason flipped his butt into a urinal. "Want to bet? Man, I used to think you were a wimp, you know? Now I know you're the biggest con man around here. You got everybody faked out, even old Gibbsy. Everybody figures you're just another jerk, huh, and you're just puttin' 'em on."

"Sure, Jason."

"'Sure, Jason,'" he jeered. "How much did *you* bet on the game? Prob'ly over five hundred."

"You're wrong."

"I can hear you lyin', man. You can con everybody else, but not me. You just think about me when you're out there tonight. Hey—I'll be rootin' for you."

He swaggered out, and after a moment I followed him. Two hundred dollars! That was another good reason to take a dive tonight. Jason got too much money from his father, but losing two hundred—after trashing the Trans Am—would make him too poor even to go for walks.

Back in the lab, I found people fooling around with the computers. Bobby Gassaway was playing a game he'd designed, naturally called UFO. It was a steal from Space Invaders, but he'd worked up some nice effects and I stopped to tell him so.

"My dad's seeing the real thing every night," Gassaway answered, pushing himself away from the keyboard and fixing his crazy eyes on me. "Last night there were three or four."

"Bull."

"Rick?" Gassaway's voice lowered confidentially. "Come on, you can tell me. How you been doing it? Balloons, or model planes, or what?"

I reached out to put a hand on the video terminal, and then changed my mind. "Gassaway," I said slowly, "I am not responsible for every glitch in your dad's radar. I haven't been doing anything except minding my own business. And lately I've got so much help from other people who want to mind my business, too, that I hardly have time to go to the john. And you've been sicking the whole damn air force on me, which is scaring my mother, and they're pestering my teachers, and—"

"What? I didn't do any of that!"

"No, you just told your dad that I must be screwing up his radar, and now I'm getting treated like some kind of spy. It'd be funny if all you clowns weren't treating it so seriously. And it's all because you're about half a bubble off plumb about flying saucers. Well, tell your dad it was all a mistake, and ask him to call off his dogs."

"My dad doesn't have anything to say about it anymore. It's at the Pentagon level now."

I gaped at him, and he looked stricken; he'd spilled the beans.

The monster in my basement wanted to punch him out. After all, Gassaway had really been more of a threat to me than Jason Murphy ever had. I resisted the urge to kill, but not because I'm such a nice guy. Gibbs was holding the interoffice phone, and looking at us.

"Stevenson."

"Sir."

"Got a minute?"

"Yes, sir."

"Good. The principal would like to chat with you."

Mr. Gordon worked in a surprisingly small cubicle tucked into one corner of the main office. He didn't have a desk, just a plain table shoved into a corner and covered with neat stacks of paper. The cubicle was just about big enough for the table, a couple of armchairs, and a couch, all surrounded by crammed bookshelves. Behind the couch, a window looked out onto a leafy green patio.

He was sitting on the couch in his shirtsleeves, reading some thick photocopied document that he seemed glad to put down.

"Hi, Rick! Have a seat." He waved me into one of the armchairs. "Care for a cup of coffee?"

"No, thank you, sir."

"Anything else? Sure? Well. I just wanted to talk for a minute before the game tonight, and wish you the best of luck. How are you feeling? Up for the game?"

"Well, kind of nervous, I guess."

"No problem. Hey, the adrenaline will give you some extra

push." Mr. Gordon folded his arms and crossed his legs and beamed at me, his freckled red face creasing like a concertina.

"You know, Rick, you're one of this school's biggest success stories. Last year we were afraid you'd run yourself into more trouble than you could handle. But you've really turned yourself around this year. John Gibbs tells me you're doing extremely well in his program, and now you're showing us what an all-rounder you are. Frankly, if someone had told me a few weeks ago that you were going to be our next big football star, I wouldn't have believed them."

"Neither would I," I agreed.

"But you know something? It's not just the brilliant football you've been playing. It's the way you've responded to your success."

"Sir?"

"Like visiting that player in the hospital. Not many people would show that kind of consideration. Don't ever lose that, huh?"

"I'll try not to, sir."

"I hope not. It shows a maturity that I wish more people had." He looked over his shoulder at the patio for a moment. "I expect this has all put a lot of stress on you."

"Oh, some."

"More than that, I'll bet. Hey, most people have a *lot* of trouble coping with, oh, fame, celebrity, whatever you want to call it. One day nobody knows you, and the next you're in the papers. It's not easy to keep your perspective."

"Well . . ."

"Have you felt a bit self-conscious lately? Kind of like a goldfish in a bowl?"

"Yes, sir. I sure have."

"Kind of puts you off stride."

So that was where he was leading. "Maybe a little, sir."

"It's showed up a bit in practice. At least to my untutored eye, you haven't had quite the bounce you had last week."

"I guess not. It doesn't worry me too much."

"Good! Good! That's the attitude. Worry about it too much and you just make everything worse. Relax. Go with the flow, as we used to say."

"I'll do my best, Mr. Gordon."

He was developing the kind of fidgets that meant the interview was nearly over, and I was eager to end it, too. But first I had to ask him something.

"Uh, sir—have a couple of guys from the air force been asking you about me?"

He had the grace to grin and shrug. "Yeah. What a laugh. Hey, they think you're fooling their radars. I told 'em that was ridiculous."

"Well, sir, to tell you the truth, that's what's been really bugging me." And I used the word "bugging" sincerely. "They really make me nervous. They even videotaped me."

"That's really pushing it. That's unacceptable. Well, I'll call the base commander and ask him to lay off our star player."

"I hope that'll work, sir. Bobby Gassaway just told me the Pentagon is involved now."

His jaw dropped; then he bristled. "I don't care if the *Kremlin* is involved. You just put it out of your mind. I'll deal with the flyboys. You might also consider the possibility that Gassaway is just embroidering on the truth a little." He looked ugly when he mentioned poor old Bobby. I guess he still remembered picking up that hot microphone and getting knocked across the main office.

"That's what I suspect, too, Mr. Gordon. But I was pretty nervous even before he told me that."

"Hey, it's okay. We'll get this all straightened out. Now I'd better let you go. We'll see you tonight, all right? Boy, I'm really looking forward to it."

Somehow I managed a grisly little smile and left. Everybody in the world seemed to be looking forward to tonight, except me.

After school, Gibbs called a short strategy meeting. He'd had his own spies out casing San Carlos, and they gave us detailed reports on what to look out for. Everybody was tense but up, eager to get at them. It even began to get to me; I recalled that I had, after all, survived the week's practices and even gained some yardage. Maybe I'd survive after all.

When the session was over, Gibbs kept me back. We were alone in the locker room, sitting on a bench in a thin mist of steam and sweat.

"Mr. Gordon tells me the Pentagon's on your case now."

"That's what Bobby told me, sir."

"Well, we took it pretty seriously. Phoned the base and talked to General Parrish, the CO. He doesn't know anything about it. Matter of fact, when I told him about your two fans from intelligence, he sounded a little embarrassed. Said they'd be reassigned right away."

"Wow!" I rocked back, slapping my hands together. "Wow, that's great. Thank you, sir."

"Glad to oblige." Gibbs leaned back against a locker and stretched out his bad leg. "You're under enough pressure without those two. I just wish you'd let up on some of the pressure you put on yourself."

"Sir?"

"You have found out something, haven't you? Like the hero of your science-fiction story. And you don't know what the heck it is, or how to handle it."

"Uh, I'm sorry, sir, but I don't think I understand."

Gibbs looked at me and smiled a little, as if he expected me to play dumb and didn't take it personally. "Stevenson, I've known you ever since you came to Terry High. You're big, and you're fairly strong, but you aren't any first-class athlete. But you discovered something that lets you perform like one. At first I thought it was some kind of drug, but anything that could speed you up like that would have bad side effects. Besides, you told me you weren't on drugs, and you were telling the truth."

I felt a strong urge to get up and run to the nearest exit. Gibbs's voice went on, calm and steady:

"That just meant you'd discovered something else. Maybe you came up with a way to increase the rate your neurons fire at, or some kind of self-hypnosis. You had that biofeedback device; maybe it's involved."

I could hardly breathe. How had he come so close?

"Whatever it is, it's got you scared and you're not using it any more. Or it's all used up. Whatever, you're just yourself again. Right?"

I stared at the floor and shrugged. "This is all just speculation, Mr. Gibbs. It's kind of funny, but that's all."

He looked a little annoyed. "Stevenson, this is not speculation. Last week I watched you run at speeds that *nobody* can reach unassisted. I worked out the speed you were traveling when you hit Al Suarez. Frankly, I'm surprised you didn't put yourself in the hospital with him. You must've been doing over thirty miles per hour when you hit Suarez."

"Aw, really, Mr. Gibbs—"

"Just for an instant, I'll grant you—which means you had some kind of jet-assist. Now, I don't like coming up with a number like thirty miles per hour, because I can't come up with a decent hypothesis to explain it. But I've observed you, and I've observed what you can do. Whatever you're doing is real. I wish it wasn't, because it disexplains so much that maybe everything I think I know about physics is wrong."

"Sir, I really don't—"

"You haven't been doing it this week, have you? Scared you might hurt somebody else like Suarez and Smith?"

"Mr. Gibbs, to tell you the truth, I'm more scared that somebody else might hurt *me.*" I laughed, trying to make it a joke, but he didn't smile.

"You've got your reasons for what you're doing, Stevenson. I have to respect them because I respect you. Now, whatever you've found out is something that makes you one hell of a football player. Without it, you're a nice guy on the third string."

I bridled at that, but Gibbs ignored my indignant expression.

"Now, I don't have room on this team for a third-stringer. If you want to get off the team, you're off. If you want to stay, I expect you to give all you've got—whatever it is."

He was giving me my freedom! I couldn't believe it. I could pack it in, walk out, and watch the game on cable television.

—But I couldn't. I'd feel like a world-historic creep. Melinda would be crushed. Pat would be worse: she'd be understanding. All the guys on the team would decide I just didn't have it. People wouldn't punch me in the arm anymore. I could go back to my job, except that Willy would wonder why I'd been such a quitter when I could've become a pro.

I wondered if this was how it felt to be corrupted: you suddenly find that something you take for granted is really important to you, so important that you're ready to sell out to keep it or get it back. Until a few days ago, being a big jock had meant nothing to me. Now I was discovering that it meant a lot, and I didn't have the guts to give it up.

"Mr. Gibbs—maybe I'm just a third-stringer, but I've been doing my best all week. At least give me this one chance, okay? Even if you only put me in for a couple of minutes, when it doesn't matter. I didn't want to be on the team at first, but now, at least I don't want to let down the other guys."

"Are you going to do your thing, or not?"

"I said I've been doing my best!" I yelled. That surprised me more than it did him. "Just don't lay any guilt trips on me, Mr. Gibbs. Let me just get through this game. And then someday maybe I can explain what this is all about."

He studied me for a moment. "All right, Stevenson. You play this game. If you don't do well you're out, and no hard feelings on either side. Deal?"

"Deal, sir." My hand disappeared inside his.

That night in the locker room everyone was blasted to bits on adrenaline and anticipation. A radio was playing loud rock, but the guys were louder. Despite all the shouting and grab-ass, we all got fitted up really fast, and stood around doing knee bends and running in place and listening to the crowd noises drifting in from outside. Across the hall, the San Carlos team was equally wound up. Finally we all lined up in the hall to get ready to run out. The San Carlos guys in their white-and-red uniforms ignored us, except for me. They looked at me a lot, their eyes bright and calculating, working out how long I'd last before they took me out of the game.

Then we heard the announcer's voice over the loud-speakers, and San Carlos went trotting out to the cheers and boos. A minute later it was our turn, and the place erupted with noise. Mr. Fogarty ran the band through a new arrangement of "When the Saints Go Marching In," with a heavy-metal quality that gave me goose pimples. Our cheerleaders, on the far side of the field, were bouncing and gyrating and whipping the crowd into a stiff meringue. Banners lashed back and forth, signs flashed under the spotlights, and somebody began cranking a siren. Talk about sensory overload! You could get the same effect by putting your head in a bucket and letting a couple of guys try to knock it off with baseball bats.

After that initial shock, the national anthem was a relief. But it didn't last long; the yelling started up again as we headed for the bench. I looked up in the stands, searching for Pat and Melinda in the mob; Melinda was there, not far from Willy Preuzer, but Pat wasn't with her. Two rows behind Melinda were Mr. Borowitz and Mr. Randall.

So much for trusting General Parrish, I thought. They were sitting there in duffel coats, one holding a video camera and the other a camera with a monster telephoto lens on it.

Those weren't the only cameras. Half a dozen photographers were standing on the sidelines, plus two camera crews from the cable company and an announcer-cameraman team from San Francisco. Flashbulbs were going off in the stands, too.

Where was Pat? I settled down on the bench, right next to Gibbs, and wondered why she wasn't with Melinda. She'd had dinner with us, and I'd driven down to school this evening thinking Pat would come with Melinda. Maybe she'd decided I might really get creamed, and didn't want to see me carried off the field like Al Suarez.

"Quit watching the crowd and pay attention to the game," Gibbs said, his voice almost inaudible under the noise.

So I sat and watched while San Carlos returned the kickoff for a touchdown. It was so fast I wasn't sure it had really happened, but then they made the conversion. Just like that, 7–0.

Well, something like that will rattle any team. We didn't let them score again in the first quarter, but we didn't exactly shine, either. It was hard, defensive football, not much fun to watch but better than getting scored against.

Early in the second quarter, San Carlos scored again. It was on a beautiful pass from their thirty-yard line. It came down into the hands of their right end, a tall black guy who outran everybody. Then they missed the conversion. We were behind 13–zip, and the crowd started yelling my number:

"Seventy-seven! Seventy-seven! Seventy-seven!"

My skin prickled, and I didn't—couldn't—turn around to look at the people in the stands. Gibbs ignored them.

We just couldn't seem to do anything right. When we got the ball, they sacked Mike Palmer. Then they intercepted a pass and ran it back almost to our end zone. We hung on, while people kept yelling, "Seventy-seven."

Sean Quackenbush came off the field and poured water all over his head as he sat next to me. Gibbs was up, limping along the sidelines and barking at people.

"Why doesn't he put you in?" Sean asked.

I just shrugged.

"Man, we gotta have you out there. They're wiping us."

Half time put us temporarily out of our misery. We shambled into the locker room and Gibbs limped up to his usual place by the blackboard.

"Gentlemen," he said quietly, "San Carlos is doing all the thinking in this game, so it's no surprise that they are dominating us. We're playing without any cohesion, without any confidence." He dissected a couple of plays, and showed everyone what had gone wrong. Then he finished up by saying: "I'm not going to waste my breath giving you a big song and dance, win this one for the Gipper, that kind of stuff. You'll win this game if you decide to win it, and I can't really influence that decision. Only you can."

"Sir?" It was Sean Quackenbush, raising his hand.

"Yes."

"Sir, can't you put in Stevenson? We really need him out there."

Gibbs looked bleak. "When I have reason to believe that Stevenson is prepared to give us a hundred-percent effort, I will put him in."

Everybody looked incredulously at me: what in the world had I done to make Gibbs say something like that?

I cleared my throat and said: "Sir, I'll do my best. But I can't promise miracles."

"Well, then," said Mike Palmer, "that oughta be good enough, Mr. Gibbs."

Gibbs studied me. "I'm not asking for miracles, Stevenson.

I don't believe in miracles. I'm just asking for whatever you've got in you."

"I'll do my best, sir," I repeated.

For a long moment, Gibbs didn't say or do anything. I began to understand the bind he was in: if he kept me on the bench he might face a mutiny from the team, but if he put me on the field I might screw up royally.

"Okay, you're in."

Everybody cheered and applauded and thumped me, and I felt surprised by the sudden change in mood. These guys really *liked* me. And I really liked them, too; I didn't want to let them down, but I didn't want to let myself down, either.

The bands finished their half time performances (ours was a lot better than theirs), and out we went again. This time the "seventy-sevens" were really loud, and a few people launched rolls of toilet paper out of the stands. When I went out onto the field, people yelled a lot and I saw the cablevision TV cameras lock on me. Mr. Borowitz and Mr. Randall were no doubt locked on me, too.

Our first chance with the ball took us well downfield on a run by Sean. As we were sorting ourselves out, a couple of San Carlos players brushed past me.

"Gonna kick your ass, man," muttered number 41. "You are goin' nowhere."

On that cheery note, I took the ball on a hand-off from Mike and ran like crazy around left end. That gained us all of three yards before they pulled me down. In the pileup, somebody gave me a knee in the kidneys.

It hurt. A lot. No one had seen it, but as I got up I saw number 41 grinning away behind his face guard. Rubbing my back, I hobbled back into the huddle. Somewhere far away the crowd was screaming a lot and the cheerleaders were doing cartwheels. For three lousy yards.

It didn't get much better; in fact, it got worse. Whenever I got the ball, the San Carlos guys just swarmed on me. On defense we did all right, and they never got close to our end zone, but we couldn't gain any yardage. When Mike tried passing to me, I couldn't get out there fast enough, except for one time when he connected and they tackled me instantly.

Near the end of the third quarter, Gibbs called me off the field. "You're trying all right," he said, "but you're just not fast enough."

I nearly mentioned the knee in the kidneys, but kept my mouth shut. My reputation with Gibbs was low enough without being a whiner.

"Give me a chance to catch my breath, Mr. Gibbs. I'll be okay."

"I'm sorry, Stevenson. We had a deal, remember? And no hard feelings."

When he said it, he sounded very sad.

I felt worse than sad. I didn't like letting him down, letting the team down. But they'd come to depend on something I couldn't deliver any more, and Gibbs was right: without it, I wasn't enough of an athlete to be much good.

The crowd didn't know that, though, and they started booing and yelling "Seventy-seven!" again. I just sat hunched inside my shoulder pads and watched as San Carlos ground away at us some more. At least, sitting on the bench, I had time to reflect on how sometimes you try to do the right thing and everything seems to go wrong.

Then the booing and yelling paused and the crowd said "Woh!" and fell silent. I couldn't understand it; nothing in particular was going on in the game. Then they said *"Woh!"* again, louder, and started clapping.

I glanced over my shoulder. Nothing much seemed to be happening, except that four cheerleaders—two girls and two guys—were going through a routine. Then I saw that the rest of the cheerleaders were just standing on the edge of the track, staring at the four with their mouths open.

It took me that long to recognize them: Eustis Bowson and Mason Reeves and Angela Battenbury and Pat Llewellyn. They were dressed just like the others, right down to the girls' tasselled boots and pleated skirts, and they were doing a pretty good job of strutting their stuff. Pat was prancing and kicking, without her brace, and when I realized that I stood up.

They got to the end of their routine, yelling, "Come on, team, give us a *goal!*" Then they all went straight up in the air about eight feet, somersaulted, and floated down like four feathers.

"Oh no. Oh no," I muttered. Gibbs, next to me, looked at me and then at the cheerleaders. He was a lot quicker to recognize them than I'd been, and his eyes widened in surprise.

I glanced away from him and looked up in the stands. Melinda was sitting there with both hands over her mouth and her eyes round. Mr. Borowitz was taping the cheerleaders and yelling something at Mr. Randall, who was clicking away with his telephoto camera and yelling back. The cable TV crews and the San Francisco cameraman were all concentrating on the cheerleaders, too.

They went into another routine that exploded into cartwheels that launched them ten feet into the air. My mouth was open as wide as anyone's and I found myself thinking that both Angela and Pat had terrific legs. And the crowd said, *"Woh-oh!"*

I threw my helmet as hard as I could onto the grass. "She planned this!" I raved, grabbing Gibbs by the arm. "She had this planned all week. She wasn't sick. None of 'em were. They were *practicing!*"

"Practicing what, Stevenson?" Gibbs asked as the four of them suddenly raced for an exit under the stands and vanished.

"Aw, Mr. Gibbs, they've blown the secret. Aw—hell!"

Gibbs grabbed me by the biceps and swung me around to face him.

"That's what I wanted out of you, Stevenson. Maybe you wanted to keep a secret for some reason, but it's no secret now. Are you going to go out there and play football?"

I was so mad and upset it took me a couple of seconds to understand what he was saying. All of a sudden I felt relaxed, easy with myself for the first time in days. I picked up my helmet.

"I might as well, Mr. Gibbs."

The game had gotten a little disorganized, because the players had seen some of the cheerleaders' stunts and couldn't believe their eyes. In the huddle, I said to Mike Palmer:

"Hand it off to me. I'm going around right end, right through that turkey who jumped on me."

Mike looked at me. "You sure you can handle him, Rick?"

"Grrrr!" I replied wittily. "Just hand me the ball, okay?"

So we set up for the play and Mike gave me the ball.

For a second there I was afraid I'd lost it forever—that I'd stand there, willing to lift myself the way I had in the kitchen that first morning, and then number 41 and his buddies would come in and puree me. But it came instantly, that funny, silent Jacuzzi feeling all over my body, and I let it rip.

My friend with the heavy kneecaps came for me, but he looked surprised at my speed. I slammed into him and nearly lost the ball, but he toppled over and I ran past him. I was in the end zone before I noticed all the cheering.

As I went trotting back down the field, the team swarmed around me. Sean gave me a hug that nearly ended my career.

"Way to *go*, man!" he bellowed. "Let's turn this game around!"

We made the conversion with no problem. Then, as we got ready to kick off to San Carlos, I looked for Pat and the others. No trace. The other cheerleaders, looking a little dazed, were bouncing up and down and yelling, "We want another one!" I looked for Melinda and the air force guys, until Gibbs roared at me to wake up and pay attention to the game.

San Carlos didn't get the ball past their own twenty-yard line; I took out their carrier. On the next down their quarterback decided to pass, and fired a long bomb. I glided backward as fast as their receiver could run forward, then lifted and intercepted. The receiver tried to grab me as I came down, but I was already long gone.

What I most remember from that play was how loud everything was. The crowd was howling, the siren was wailing, and my own breath roared in my ears. San Carlos came at me. I headed for one guy at a high rate of speed and he flinched and dropped, trying to snag me around the ankles as I went past. Instead, I bounced a couple of feet into the air and went on through.

So now it was 13–all. The noise of the crowd built up, aided by the two bands, until Mike Palmer made the conversion and took us ahead 14–13.

I'll say this for San Carlos: they never quit. By the end of the game the score was 28–13, but they were still in there. We

all shook hands and I turned to look for Pat again. The crowd
was coming out onto the field, or heading for the exits, when
somebody screamed.

That was some scream; it froze several thousand people
right in their tracks. I saw somebody point upward, and
looked up also.

Descending out of the darkness into the floodlights were
Pat and Angela and Eustis and Mason. Eustis was carrying an
American flag in one of those straps; he'd probably swiped it
from somebody in the band. The four of them came down in a
kind of diamond pattern, with Pat closest to the Terry High
stand and Eustis farthest away. Pat was carrying a bullhorn,
and when they got about twenty feet from the ground they
leveled off and she put it to her mouth.

"Good evening, ladies and gentlemen!" she said. "My
name is Pat Llewellyn, and you are witnessing a demonstra-
tion of a newly discovered physical phenomenon called lifting."

The field full of football players, the stands full of spectators—everyone fell dead silent. There they hovered, four kids
in blue-and-gold cheerleaders' outfits, with the flag flapping
around Eustis's face.

"We can't explain it all," Pat went on, her voice echoing
against the stands. "But we can tell you that this is no joke.
It's a skill that just about anybody can learn, and starting
tomorrow we're going to teach it to anybody who asks. Now,
I'd like you to give a big hand to the guy who first discovered
lifting—number seventy-seven, Rick Stevenson!"

I wish I could say they gave me a standing ovation, but all
they did was clap slowly, like a bunch of hypnotized seals.
Gibbs looked at me with a vindicated expression on his grinning face—another hypothesis confirmed.

Pat lowered her bullhorn and grinned down at me. "Hey,
come on up, Rick. The view is really fine up here."

I looked at Gibbs again, grinned self-consciously, and
handed my helmet to Mike Palmer. "Back in a minute," I
mumbled, and lifted to join her. Eustis and Mason and Angela
closed in around us, hugging us and laughing.

"You shoulda seen your face, man!" Eustis crowed. "You

looked over your shoulder and nearly fell off the bench."

"You sneaky rat," I said to Pat. "You faked me out completely. I'm gonna get you for this."

She laughed, and it was a burst of music. The floodlights made her hair glitter, and her hazel eyes gleamed. "Have to catch me first!"

Dropping her bullhorn, Pat soared up into the darkness beyond the floodlights. Growling and laughing, I followed her up.

Later we would have to come back down and explain all kinds of things to Melinda and Gibbs and Mr. Borowitz and Mr. Randall and the TV crews. We would be stuck in the floodlights for a long time, maybe the rest of our lives, and that wouldn't always be fun.

With the wind in my face, I tried to decide how I felt. Was I angry? Well, I had been when Pat and the others had first started their cheerleading routine, but I realized the monster in my basement hadn't even twitched. I suspected the stupid critter had slept through everything. Maybe, if I smartened up enough, he'd sleep forever.

Was I scared? Sort of. But seeing the Awkward Squad float down out of the darkness had made me realize what I should've realized from the moment I taught Pat: nobody owns freedom, and nobody can give it away, either. Each of us takes it, as much as we can handle and usually a little more, and if we screw it up we can't blame anybody but ourselves. Maybe I had taught her, but I still hadn't learned what Gibbs had been trying so hard to teach us all: to be grown-up enough not to need other people to tell us what to do.

Once Pat could lift, she could make up her own mind what to do about it. I could argue with her, but I couldn't force her to do what I wanted. Lifting could make you free only if you were ready to think and act for yourself, and ready to let others do the same. Pat had been and I hadn't. I hadn't trusted myself and I hadn't trusted her or anybody else—yet somehow I'd hoped that somebody else would make decisions for me. If everybody could lift, and some people misused their new freedom to hurt other people, it wouldn't be my fault. The rest of us would have to deal with them—and what we did about it couldn't be my decision alone.

Was I sad? I knew I was going to miss the specialness of being alone in the sky with Pat. Before long, we would be just two more ordinary people out of millions or billions who could lift as well as we did. We'd be special only in the ways we'd been before—stupid-smart, severely gifted, basically pretty nice people. That would have to be enough.

I wasn't going to enjoy everything that happened after this, like Jason winning his bet and Gassaway yelling that he'd been right all along. But some things I knew I was going to like a lot—like teaching Melinda and Gibbs and his wife and girls how to lift.

That could all wait a little longer. For now, it was enough just to rise swiftly toward the stars, following Pat's laughter into the moonlit night.

295

MORE SCIENCE FICTION ADVENTURE!